Praise for
flies *on the* butter

"A poignant southern tale of how the lost can find their way back home. And how deep roots and southern memories—like chocolate pie, boiled peanuts, and crazy waitresses in small town diners—can remind you of why sometimes life has to come to a screeching halt so we can learn how to live."

—christianbookpreviews.com

"*Flies on the Butter* would be an excellent book for a lazy afternoon when you want to be entertained and even feel touched."

—epinions.com

Flies on the Butter is a 2007 Pulpwood Queen selection.

Other Books by Denise Hildreth

Savannah from Savannah
Savannah Comes Undone
Savannah by the Sea

flies *on the* butter

denise hildreth

THOMAS NELSON
Since 1798

NASHVILLE   DALLAS   MEXICO CITY   RIO DE JANEIRO   BEIJING

This book is dedicated to anyone who
has needed to find their way back home.

And to my older brother, Darren—
here's to remembering all the lizards still
running around without their tails.

———

Copyright © 2007 by Denise Hildreth

Published in Nashville, Tennessee by Thomas Nelson. Thomas Nelson is a trademark of Thomas Nelson, Inc.

Thomas Nelson, Inc. titles may be purchased in bulk for educational, business, fund-raising, or sales promotional use. For information, please e-mail SpecialMarkets@ThomasNelson.com.

Publisher's Note: This novel is a work of fiction. Names, characters, places, and incidents are either products of the author's imagination or used fictitiously. All characters are fictional, and any similarity to people living or dead is purely coincidental.

Library of Congress Cataloging-in-Publication Data

Hildreth, Denise, 1969-
  Flies on the butter / Denise Hildreth.
     p. cm.
  ISBN-13: 978-1-59554-208-3 (pbk.)
  ISBN-10: 1-59554-208-6 (pbk.)
  1. South Carolina—Fiction. I. Title.
PS3608.I424F55 2007
813'.6—dc22   2006031511

Printed in the United States of America
07 08 09 10 11 RRD 9 8 7 6 5 4 3

1

S he's here. She got in about an hour ago," Charlotte said, her gum popping audibly over the phone. Rose was sure it was pink. The gum, that is.

Tension sank into Rose's back as quickly as a pig into mud. She started tapping the steering wheel with her right hand. "You're sure?"

"Am I sure? Oh no, forgive me. It's not your mother that just walked through the door. No, oh my goodness. No, I think I was completely wrong. Well, I'll be. It's Flora Mae Jacobson, Suge's sister, from the family who obviously has a fondness for baking products. How could I have been so blind? . . . Of course it's your mother, Rosey."

"Charlotte, please."

"Oh, I'm sorry . . . Of course it's your mother, *Rose*. Now, why exactly did you want me to call you and let you know when she got here? You're going to have to see her whether you like it or not."

Rose knew it was true. She'd simply felt that she wouldn't have to officially begin dreading every aspect of this trip home until the exact moment her mother arrived. *Welcome to that moment.* "What's she doing now?"

"Scrubbing the countertop in the kitchen. So all the food that's arriving soon can just dirty it all up again."

Rose's mother had been scrubbing things for years. Trying to clean away her guilt since Rose was twelve.

"How much longer till you get here?"

"I just left."

"You just left?" The drawl in her cousin's voice escalated. As if that were possible for a girl capable of winning the "Talks So Southern She Sound Likes a Foreigner" contest. "You said you were leaving by seven."

"I left at seven fifteen."

"Well, Uncle JT and Aunt Claudine are going to be here around noon, and then Aunt Nella and Uncle Wusser are coming shortly thereafter."

Rose was certain that her mamaw's labor pains had been so intense that they were the reason for her judgment paralysis when it came to naming her children. Obviously the worse-than-normal labor pains were epidemic in that region.

"So please hurry. Until you or your brother gets here, I'm forced to endure these crazy people all alone."

"Isn't your brother there?"

"Like I said . . ."

Rose laughed. "Well, I talked to Christopher this morning. He should be there any minute. I mean, craziness does deserve company."

"Well, I don't deserve craziness. Maybe a bus ticket to the pit of wickedness—at least according to people's evaluations of me around here—but I don't deserve craziness."

"Hang in there. I'll be there in ten hours, give or take an hour." Rose didn't plan to break records to get home.

"We're all going to see Mamaw when you get here."

"How about I just meet you there." It wasn't a question.

"That's not in your mother's plan. She has us all driving over together so you can catch up with your family."

Rose's mother had been reaching out to her with endless effort. Each attempt hit Rose's brick wall and bounced back. "Like I said, I'll just meet you there."

"You can avoid, but you cannot hide." Rose's mother's shame only ran so deep. "She *will* have all of us together for dinner."

The steering wheel's leather seemed to meld underneath Rose's fingernails. "That's fine," she said, knowing that there would be multiple red and white buckets with a smiling old man on the front. She wouldn't touch the stuff. "Well, I need to go. I have another call coming in. Thanks for letting me know."

———~———

Rose didn't check the caller ID on the display screen of her dashboard before pressing the small telephone icon that was built into her steering wheel and settled nicely beneath her thumb.

"Rose Fletcher."

"Rose, it's Helen. Did you finish that proposal?" Rose felt her shoulders loosen. Work. This was a world she knew, understood, could control. "This job, not to mention this city, waits for nothing and no one. Neither does Max."

She smiled at Helen's stubbornness. Helen wasn't scared of a thing, but Rose's boss, Max, drove Helen right close to the edge of insanity. And even drove her to drink a time or two, if Rose was correct about the contents of the little metal flask Helen kept in the back of her top filing drawer.

"Yes. I left it on his desk. Tell him it's resting safely underneath his Cuban cigar box."

She was certain of the smile that graced Helen's face. That was the perfect place to leave something for Max—right under his faithful companions of late-night work. Rose had even shared a few cigars with him over the years. "Ooh, that was perfect."

"Well, I knew it would be *perfectly* safe there."

"So how long are you going to be gone exactly?" Rose

knew Helen's brow was now furrowed, a brow she said Botox would never be allowed to touch. When Max informed her there was "stuff for those kinds of things now," she'd scoffed, "I worked hard for these wrinkles."

"You don't take vacations, remember," Helen continued.

"I assure you, this isn't a vacation. I'm just going to take care of some business back at home. But I'll just be a few days." Rose hesitated, then forced herself back to the conversation. "This is something I have to do."

"Well, that's neither here nor there. Plus the coffeepot broke, and I doubt I'm even going to stay much longer myself. I can't work with these slave drivers around here and not get my recommended dose of caffeine."

Rose had sworn off caffeine.

"Well, I'm sure we'll be talking a thousand times. But you better appreciate me even more when you return, because your absence means Max is hounding me instead of you."

"I don't mind. But quit biting your nails."

"How did you—?"

Rose laughed. "You always bite your nails when you talk about Max. Anyway, call me whenever you need to. It'll make the drive go quicker, if that's possible."

"Well, you drive careful now. If anything happened to you, Max would throw himself out his own window. He knows who does the work while he gets the big office. And why are you driving anyway? Hello, take a flight, why don't you?"

If Rose had any doubts before why Helen kept a notepad by her side all day, she had no doubts now. Helen had ADD.

"I'm going to South Carolina, Helen, not Mexico. Plus, I need to clear my head before I get there. I can't do that on a plane."

"Yeah, clear your head my wrinkled booty. We both know why you don't fly."

"And why is that, oh Wise One?"

"Because that would mean you aren't the one behind the wheel. Too much loss of control. Ooh, I gotta go. Max is hollering at me."

Rose opened her mouth to counter such a statement, but Helen was gone.

"Nice to talk to you too," Rose said to the car phone. It didn't respond.

───~───

The last line of the Wynonna song sifted through the car: "You can dream about it every now and then. But you can't go home *again*."

"You've got that right," Rose said as she pressed the search button—also integrated into her steering wheel, along with the volume, the cruise control, and other features. Eventually she found a light jazz station, and the mellow saxophone playing helped her relax.

She took a drink of the bottled water she'd brought along.

The yellow line that continually blurred on the pavement outside her window reminded her that she had a long drive ahead of her. And the ten-hour trek to her mamaw's only provided an excessive amount of time to dwell on the craziness that would await her. Going back to the place of your roots and seeing family had a way of dredging up memories—not always pleasant ones.

"Not that South Carolina is home anymore," she assured herself and adjusted her seat position to be more comfortable. No, South Carolina might be home to the first battle of the Civil War and the largest ginkgo farm in the world, but it wasn't her home anymore.

She knew every member of her mother's family would be in Mullins, South Carolina, by the time she got there. That's what events like this brought. And Southern people look for an excuse to celebrate just about anything. But Rose wasn't sure they considered her that much a part of the family anymore, not that she cared. After all, she was the only one bold enough, as they called her, to move so far from home.

Besides, apparently she wasn't the only one moving away from Mullins, because in the last three years, the population had decreased from 5,910 to 4,854. The murder rate was still at zero, however, so at least Rose didn't have to worry that they were being killed off one by one.

The sleepy town in the heart of the Deep South was named for Colonel William S. Mullins, a railroad president and representative of Marion County in the South Carolina Legislature from 1852 to 1866. But it really came into existence in the 1600s, when farming families began to call this rural town home. Mullins was formally established in 1872, with fewer than a hundred people and nothing more than four streets and three stores.

But the tobacco market arrived in 1894, and everything changed. Tobacco was the official occupation of Rose's family. The Mullins Tobacco Market sold more tobacco than any other market in the state, and it was the main reason Mullins's population grew at all. Of course, Mamaw and Granddaddy's reproduction rate didn't hurt the population. With nine children, a few more sons- and daughters-in-law than children, and enough grandchildren to start their own church, the jolly clan was a strong force in the tiny town.

And that entire clan would want Rose's visit—along with the visits of others who would be coming in from different parts of the state—to be a time of catching up. She sighed. Southerners' ideas of catching up were about nothing more than new revelations of craziness. At least according to the dictionary of Rose. And she didn't need any more of that. She had never understood how such complete dysfunction could come from two beautiful people like her grandparents. But it had.

And she couldn't help but reflect on the fact that she had come from her mother.

The hectic traffic of Alexandria, Virginia, was at its peak at this time of the morning. Though Rose's car was barely moving, the December winter winds blew furiously around it, making it clear to fall that it was no longer welcome. But despite its harsh winters, Washington DC had been kind to Rose. It had given her community. The kind that gets close but not too close. It had given her a good living. And a nice house. And a husband. No children, though.

Her e-mail beeped.

Rose had spent years talking on her cell phone and checking her Palm, all while driving. But because of life's ever-increasing efficiency, she now had a BlackBerry, which combined all these functions into one piece of technology. She loved it.

Rose opened the e-mail. *Breakfast meeting with your opposition at 8:00 a.m. on Wednesday. When you whup up on them, every student and teacher in the state will love you! Helen.* She had added a smiley face. The woman loved emoticons.

A nearby car honked, and Rose swerved. She set the BlackBerry on the seat beside her, deciding that arriving home in one piece would be best. As if that were possible.

She was certain Helen would drive her crazy all day. But she didn't care. Despite the age difference, Helen was her closest friend these days. If you called interaction from nine to five a friendship. Because Helen didn't work past five. But Rose didn't have much time for anyone else.

A traffic light flashed in front of her. She stopped before the on ramp to the interstate that would carry her home . . . well, not home, but back to the place of her birth.

———

"Red light, green light." The words came fast and furious from Rosey's cousin Bobby Dean.

"Rosey, you have to stop when they say, 'Red light,'" her brother, Christopher, scolded, refusing to hide his irritation. Three and a half years older, and with brown eyes that matched hers, he had become her favorite playmate.

"I did stop," she declared firmly, flinging her auburn locks across one shoulder. Her bare foot slapped the cracked concrete walkway as she placed her hands adamantly on the sides of her khaki shorts. Bobby Dean didn't let the protest sidetrack him. "Yellow light . . . yellow light . . . yellow light . . . RED LIGHT!"

Rosey teetered on her pencil-thin legs as she brought her weight to an immediate halt. She kept her eye on the finish line—the front set of stairs to Mamaw and Granddaddy's wraparound front porch.

"I don't like that red-light part!" Bobby Dean's sister, Charlotte, protested in Southern linguistics. (That's where perfectly good words with one syllable take two.)

"You don't like anything," retorted Bobby Dean.

"I was almost at the front of the line! You did it on purpose. Mama!" And with that Charlotte ran away to the world of her mama's consolation.

"Go! Go!" Rosey demanded.

"Green light," the conductor resumed. "Green light . . ."

"I won!" Rosey declared, throwing up her hands in victory and doing a little jig up and down the steps. The wooden planks of her grandparents' porch were splintering on the ends where the ancient nails were giving up their battle to hold them in place, but her bare feet danced without incident. Until she ran smack-dab into her dad, who had come up the side set of stairs to the porch.

"Whoa there, baby girl!" He scooped her up and gave her a hug as her mama came up behind him with a smile. "I didn't get a kiss from you this morning," her daddy said, kissing her face in quick pecks amid her giggles.

"Oh, Daddy. We had a busy day." She wrapped her arms around his neck and kissed him back.

"You did?" He laughed and placed her back down on the porch. He took her mama by the hand. "Well, your mama and I are going inside to have lunch with Mamaw and Granddaddy."

"You and Christopher need to come in shortly, Rosey honey, and get you something to eat too," her mama added with her own kiss to Rosey's forehead.

"We got more playing to do." She narrowed her eyes at Bobby Dean, who had just sat down on a step.

"Well, Rosey," added her daddy, "all that playing will require energy. So don't forget to eat."

"Sure, sure, Daddy," she reassured him with a few pats and returned her attention to her brother. "Okay, let's play Giant Steps! Okay, let's, let's!" Rosey said, clapping and bouncing up and down.

Christopher ignored the request and, scooting one of Mamaw's pots from its resting place at the edge of the walkway, sat down next to Bobby Dean. Roly-polies scrambled in desperate search of new cover.

"Ooh, I love those," Rosey said, leaning over Christopher's shoulder to get a better look.

He flicked her hair out of his face. Then he picked up a roly-poly. Rosey watched in fascination as it promptly rolled into a ball to protect itself.

"Can I hold it? Please?" Rosey asked, extending her light brown hand. According to her daddy, her "rich olive complexion" came courtesy of her daddy's mother, who was part Cherokee Indian.

Christopher set the roly-poly gently into her palm. Okay, well, he had shown her the world these first five years of her life—introduced her to climbing trees, making mud pies, and getting soybeans from the neighbor's farm to make their own concoctions—he might as well show her this. "Okay, Rosey, just take it and roll it around in your hand."

Rosey's brow furrowed as she held out both hands to obey.

Bobby Dean elbowed her. "Lighten up, Rosey. You look as serious as my mama on salon day."

She elbowed him back. Harder.

She turned her attention back to her latest discovery. "Why does it roll up like that?"

"To protect itself," Christopher said and then picked up another one. Bobby Dean reached over him to retrieve his own prize as well.

"To protect itself from what?"

"To protect itself from you!" Bobby Dean retorted.

Rosey crinkled her nose and wiped a hanging curl from her eye, depositing a streak of mud across her forehead. "But I wouldn't hurt it," she said, carefully rolling it around in her hand with her index finger. "I wouldn't hurt it for the world. I would never hurt anything, Christopher."

⁓

A horn honked long and loud. Rose registered that the light had turned green. She was tired of horns already.

"Get a grip, woman! The light just turned green." Rose cursed as she put her foot on the gas and merged onto the interstate.

If Rose's mamaw had heard those words come out of her mouth, she would have marched Rose straight to the church next door and baptized her in the name of the Father, the Son, and the Holy Spirit. And she would have dunked her with each name just to make sure it took. But Rose would offer the driver behind her no mercy. With Rose, mercy was an ever decreasing commodity.

The green of the interstate sign that sped by her window at eighty miles an hour caused her to reach for the green folder she had brought along. She needed to make a few phone calls to the opposition to ensure their compliance. But the passenger seat held no green folder. She refused to panic. She snatched her fifteen-hundred-dollar handbag, a gift to herself, from the floorboard of the car, and there was still no green.

"You have got to be kidding me!" she yelled over the background music. Then she sighed in disgust.

That's when she remembered. Even now she could see the green folder on the back of the caramel-hued velvet sofa that she and Jack had purchased their first year of marriage. She had perfectly positioned it there and left it for the purpose of making it unavoidable as she walked out the door. But then Christopher had called to soothe her regarding the destination to come. He knew she'd need soothing, and she was, as always, grateful for it. So how could she blame him? Besides, something more unavoidable than green on caramel had distracted her: the wedding picture on the bookcase nestled between the windows in the family room. She had picked it up slowly. Tried to push the aching back to the recesses of her mind, where it belonged. The never-talked-about aches. The un-noticed ones. Until something forced you to notice.

Glimpsing Jack's face in the picture this morning was what had caused her to pick up the photo. She hadn't seen that face on him in a long time. The youthfulness in his eyes had turned older. The beautiful smile had been replaced with a solemnness she'd never known was in him. For a moment this morning, she had ached.

But not for long. Rose never ached for long. So she laid the picture facedown. She didn't want to have to look at it when she got home. Then she walked out, fortified by her statement to the world and to herself . . . and left her green folder perfectly positioned for her distracted eye.

Remembering it all now made her fume even more. She accelerated the car to eighty-five. And blue lights soon followed close behind.

2

Do you know how fast you were going, ma'am?" the police officer asked after striking an official pose beside her window and seeming not to notice that Rose's window was still rolled up. She read his lips.

Rose cut the radio off and glared at him as she rolled the window down, freezing wind sweeping into the warm vehicle. That caused her to roll the window only halfway down. Well, that was part of the reason. "You caught me," she said, "so not fast enough."

The muscle in his jaw twitched. "License and registration . . . *please.*"

She reached to open the glove compartment. That was about the only thing in her new Lexus GS300 that didn't operate itself or talk to her. She'd bought the Lexus right off the showroom floor. It made her feel special. The engine started simply by pushing a button. Air-conditioning blew air up through the seat and cooled off her behind. Now, that was an offering most would have no idea they even needed until they had it. The sedan was painted charcoal gray, and the same hue was inside, with black accents. It was powerful, making the statement she wanted it to make. Though unfortunately today it made the statement, "Pull me over, please. I'm a power machine."

Rose extended her license and registration through the narrow opening, suppressing a shiver.

The officer took them and said, "I'll be back in a—" She rolled up her window before he could finish.

She sat there on the side of the interstate, watching the motorists who passed by watch her. Each one breathing a sigh of relief, she knew, thankful that they weren't her. And if she were being completely honest, she would say there were probably days she desired the very same thing herself.

"You really need to slow down, ma'am," the officer said when he returned and she had rolled the window down slightly again. Her declaration of defiance. "This is a weapon you have here."

Rose scanned the officer, meeting his gaze for the first time. "May I go now?"

He gave her back her documents, along with a ticket. "Yes, you can go. But please be careful. No one else on the highway deserves other drivers to be distracted. And by the way you were floating all over the road, I'd say you are way too distracted today."

She rolled up her window without offering another word. She merged back onto the highway and, going the speed limit, tapped her cruise-control button to keep herself from getting another ticket. She crossed her right leg over her left, leaving the accelerator free. It was the position she had assumed through the years for comfort on monotonous car trips. Well, as monotonous as a ten-hour road trip with a speeding ticket in the first thirty minutes could be.

———~———

"So, Rosey, what's the actual amount of time a person should be forced to endure craziness?" Charlotte complained in her rich drawl, the sounds of craziness echoing in the background. "Crap! I didn't mean to call you Rosey. It's just such a habit. Why did you have to go and change your name anyway?"

"CHARLOTTE! DON'T YOU SAY 'CRAP' IN THIS HOUSE AGAIN," Rose heard Charlotte's mother scold.

"A thirty-two-year-old woman still being scolded by her mother. What a sad life I have."

"Join the sad-luck club. I just got pulled over." She didn't try to conceal her agitation.

Charlotte barked her unmistakable laugh—half hyena, half snort. "You always were dangerous behind the wheel."

Rose couldn't help but laugh at Charlotte's laugh. Come to think of it, she'd laughed at Charlotte most of her life. Charlotte was the vanilla to her strawberry, as her daddy called them. They were more alike than Rose would ever admit. Because Charlotte was a continual reminder of what Rose ran from. The Southern mind-set. The Southern perception. The Southern lifestyle. At least the lifestyle Rose still perceived the South to have. But they were alike in so many ways that they couldn't help but like each other. And even though Rose had run from so much, Charlotte always reached out to pull her back home.

"You remember that time you completely convinced Uncle Junior that you could drive?"

Rose scanned her memory. "Oh my word. I'd completely forgotten about that. What were we? Thirteen?"

"You were thirteen. I was twelve." Charlotte loved to remind Rose that she was older, especially the older they got.

"We had ordered a pizza from Pizza Hut, hadn't we?"

"Yeah, and you told him that you had your driver's license." She snorted again.

"It did take me awhile to convince him, though. I think he even followed us."

Smack and snort. "He did. He knew we were lying through our teeth."

"I can't believe we made it home alive. Because when I had to make that left turn at that huge intersection, I scared myself to death."

"Get yourself outta here, girlfriend! I don't buy that for a second, Rose Fletcher. You've never been scared of anything."

Rose half chuckled to herself. Little did she know. Little did she know.

———

"And it was sooooooo dark." Christopher's voice tremored.

Rosey dug her head farther under the covers.

"And they heard him outside, saying, 'I'm going to get you.'" He leaned his mouth closer to where her head was hidden.

"I don't want to hear anymore, Christopher!" Her muffled cries came from under the comforter. "It's too scary."

"And then"—his voice grew softer, more evil sounding— "they finally got the car running and sped out of the creaky old park. And when they got home"—Rosey whimpered— "they found his hook attached to the door handle."

Well, that was the final straw. Rosey took off like a streak, screaming in fitful tears as she ran into the family room. Her mama and daddy were curled up on the sofa, watching television. "Chris . . . he . . . hook . . ." She gasped for air, trying to get the words out. Her little body was shaking as though she had found the hook herself.

Her daddy wrapped her in his arms as she buried her face in his neck. "Did Christopher scare my baby?"

"Bad, Daddy, bad . . ." She continued to cry.

"The one-armed monster will take care of him," he

assured her as he sat her down on the sofa, underneath her mama's waiting arm.

Rosey could still hear Christopher's laughter. He had plumb near made himself slaphappy. She knew he hated her being in his bed. But she liked it better than her own.

She was in the family room, still cowering beneath her mother's arm, when she and her mama heard rustling outside Christopher's window, followed by his screams, and then came the streak of his body as he ran through the kitchen, in their direction. Her poor brother planted his head in the seat of Daddy's recliner as if that would prevent the wicked one-armed monster from finding him.

The one-armed monster returned via the back sliding glass doors and looked pretty much slaphappy himself. Once Christopher realized that the noise was only his father's retribution, he gathered his nerves and went back to bed. Back to bed, with Rosey curled up beside him. This time he actually let her.

And Rosey would spend the rest of her life being scared. Only years down the road, the monsters became real.

———

"So no more lead foot," Charlotte stated. "Did you hear me?"

Rose caught sight of the road before her and wondered what all had transpired while her thoughts had been somewhere else. Another world. "No more lead foot," she assured.

"So how is everybody doing, you know, with all the emotion that surrounds an event like this?"

"Everybody is waiting on you to get here. Well, you and Aunt Lavernia. You know that woman is slower than a turtle on Valium. We'll probably still be waiting on her by the time the last bite of pound cake is eaten. But trust me, as soon as you get here, we're all going to see Mamaw together. But we want to see you in one piece. There's enough going on around here without adding you to our worry list."

Rose knew what she meant and how she meant it. "Don't worry, I won't be demanding anyone's attention this weekend. This is about Mamaw and Mamaw alone."

"Everyone will be glad to see you. You don't need to worry."

Rose said good-bye. And she wasn't worried. She wasn't worried about how her family felt about seeing her. No, that wasn't the real issue on her mind.

———

She clicked on the radio to destroy the silence. Silence made Rose uncomfortable. She was too good at talking, anyway, to enjoy silence. Rush Limbaugh's voice came through the speakers. Rose listened to everything. Information was Rose's friend when it came to her job and her life. And she was so good at what she did and at making people feel comfortable that each side of the aisle was convinced she had voted for the one on the other. Because of that, Washington's regard for her was growing.

She had gone to the College of Charleston her freshman year, while her brother, Christopher, was finishing his senior year at the Citadel. When he graduated, she decided she would rather make a life for herself in the North, so with her 4.0 she transferred to the more liberal Brown University in Rhode Island to try to get away from the South and its backwoods and chewing tobacco and talking in a way that left off the last letter of the word. Like *wantin'*, *somethin'*, *watchin'*, *gonna*—well, that word they just changed altogether.

Basically, Rose ran from what she had come from and made herself what she had become. A professional advocate for children who was taken seriously and respected immensely. The years of Northern dialect, as well as her own determination, had removed most of her Southern drawl. But sometimes when she was excited or wasn't thinking, it sneaked up on her. Yet as soon as someone noted the accent as "cute," she snapped it back into shape and commanded it to obey. It did. All things she commanded obeyed. Well, maybe not all.

But Rose had flourished in Washington. The National Education Center had recruited her from the public relations firm she'd joined right out of college. Her gift for communication and the art of persuasion provided teachers and children with one of the most effective mouthpieces Washington had seen in awhile. She was Max's star pupil.

A beep came from her BlackBerry on the passenger seat, alerting her to a new e-mail. She loved having everything in one handy device. She pressed the *open* button.

I have a few questions about the lunch tomorrow. Call me after you've viewed the attachment. Helen.

Rose's car swerved. She decided against opening the attachment right now.

She clicked the radio off and entered Helen's number on her Blackberry. The car phone wouldn't let her dial while the car was in motion. Obviously manufacturers had heard about drivers like her. But her BlackBerry's Bluetooth allowed calls to be heard through the car phone.

"Rose Fletcher's office," came Helen's voice through the speakers.

"Hey, Helen. What's up?"

"Have you ever wondered why people feel the need to pierce their tongues?"

"Does this have anything to do with the lunch tomorrow?" Rose inquired.

"No, absolutely nothing, but it has everything to do with the strange-looking creature that just brought me my coffee." Rose heard her slurp. "Okay, now my brain can officially function."

Rose shook her head.

"I just wanted to make sure you got the update I just received from Senator Waterstone."

Rose heard the shuffling papers. "No, I haven't opened it yet. I've taken to not reading my e-mails while I'm driving. I think it might be best."

"Already gotten a ticket?" Helen always knew. "I told you about that, Rose. If you don't slow up, you're going to wrap yourself around a tree. Not that I'm trying to put that mojo on you or anything, but I've ridden with you. Honey, I almost went out and bought me some Depends in case I ever had to do that again."

Rose laughed. "Helen, you're too young for Depends," she assured her.

"You're too kind—but also a liar. I guess all that Clairol is working. Do you think the black's too harsh for my skin tone?"

She would ask until Rose answered. "No. It's the perfect complement."

"It never comes out quite like the bottle. Of course, those faces have ten years on me."

Rose wouldn't laugh, even though she knew those faces had thirty years on her. Yet Helen called Rose the old soul.

"Now, stop distracting me and read that e-mail as soon as you stop."

"I'll be stopping soon to get a bite to eat anyway. I can look over it then. I guess this means that my breakfast companions and I will have even more to talk about next week." A sly smile touched her lips. She relished the verbal negotiation.

"I'm sure they're looking *so* forward to having breakfast with you."

Rose sat up straighter in the car seat and decided she liked the position of power. "I guess I'll have to make a few phone calls beforehand, won't I?"

"You do have a way with senators," Helen replied with a reprimand in her voice.

"Helen," Rose scolded.

"Well, say what you will, but not only did he send the memo this morning, which reveals that the opposition must be waffling"—she didn't allow Rose to respond about this irritating development—"but he also called for you *again* this morning. Something about wanting to make sure your calendar was clear for this Monday and Tuesday. He said he'd called you but kept getting your voice mail. He figured you were on the phone or something. I told him you were having to go home because of an event in your family and that you should be back sometime over the weekend. And oddly enough"—the inflection in her voice grew in concern again—"he seemed to know you were going home."

Rose didn't comment. Neither would her senator.

3

The bottled water Rose had consumed needed liberation. A rest area sign indicated that her goal was one mile ahead. It couldn't come soon enough. She remembered the last time the surging need had her heading to the restroom so quickly that she missed seeing the skirted stick figure icon and walked in on Congressman Watley. He had his back to her and was donning his baby blue sport coat. She screamed, "Don't turn around!" to his startled expression in the mirror and abruptly reversed direction. Since then, word had gotten out that Rose Fletcher would follow a person anywhere to get her job accomplished. She didn't really mind such talk.

Rose pulled into a parking place as close to the facilities as possible. She put the car in park, then took her coffee-colored cashmere shawl from the passenger's seat, letting the softness glide underneath her fingertips. She wrapped it around her shoulders and raised it gently to her face. Its familiarity soothed her as much as its warmth shielded her. She climbed from the car and walked quickly up the walkway. She shivered. A man holding the hand of a little girl no older than three opened the door so she could come inside.

"Can you say 'excuse me' to the nice lady?" the young man said to his little one as he pulled her hood up over her head.

"Excuse me, nice lady," the child replied obediently, tilting her head up and letting a smile of tiny teeth peek out from underneath her hood.

"Why, thank you, little miss." Rose grinned back at her. The father laughed as he scooped up his little girl. He peppered her face with kisses as he carried her to the car. Rose could hear the child's giggles even after the restroom door closed. The little girl's spirit was contagious, and for a moment, Rose felt lighter. But only for a moment. Quickly her smile faded. And she tried to push back the thoughts of Jack and children as they forced their way into her thoughts. She had far too much to think about to let her mind navigate those waters today. And after all, she was taking good care of children. That should be enough.

The car still held its heat, and Rose was thankful. Hopefully, as she drove farther south, the icy bite would leave the air.

Nothing she could do about the bite in her gut that would only increase at the thought of getting closer to her mother. But there was something she could do about the bite in her gut from her opposition. She dialed a telephone number on the dashboard electronic screen that, among other functions, calculated miles, adjusted temperatures, and showed current CD selections. She put the car in reverse and listened as the ringing came from the other end.

"Senator Tomason's office," the refined voice answered. Rose made a note to have Helen call this number a couple of times and listen to how this lady answered the telephone. Of course, by the time Helen finished throwing the phone at her, they both would have forgotten what she had even asked her to do.

"Senator Tomason, please. Would you let him know Rose Fletcher with the National Education Center is calling?"

"One moment, ma'am."

The hold music tried to soothe her. You'd expect "The Star-Spangled Banner" or something, but this was a nice alternative. But waiting didn't soothe her. And the senator was making her wait. Rose wasn't impressed. All senators and congresspeople liked people to think they were busy and important. And both seemed to go hand in hand. Yet even senators knew it was people like Rose who got the most accomplished within that chamber.

"Well, well . . . Rose Fletcher. To what do I owe the privilege this morning?"

Rose put on her game face, or in this case, her phone voice. "Senator Tomason, it's a pleasure to find you available this morning. Thanks so much for taking some time to chat."

"I always have time to chat with you, Rose. You know that." He laid on the Southern charm strong enough to tie a noose.

"Well, I got word this morning that there might be a slight snag in our education bill. And I would just hate to think that all of those fine teachers wouldn't be able to get their needs met in this upcoming year because we had a communication problem. So if I've made something unclear in this bill, something that doesn't satisfy you, then I'd love to get your thoughts so we can correct it."

"Well, you know, Rose,"—she could imagine his heavy, round frame leaning back in his chair as he rubbed his belly like a genie—"I've got some constituents who are really concerned about this bill. So I think we might need to look at it again and make some revisions."

Rose tried to squelch her seething. She had worked on this bill for months. It would be one of her greatest accomplishments to date, and just a week ago, Senator Tomason had okayed it for his side, making it as official as anything in Washington ever really was. "Well, I understand, but I thought we had your support. At least that's the impression you left me with last week."

"Well now, Rose, you need to understand this is an election year. And I can't be ticking off my faithful constituents with a bill that they're just not real happy about . . ." He paused to gauge her response. She didn't respond. She knew he'd have a "but." They always had a "but." "But you know, Rose, if your education group wants to think about this further, with *it* being an election year and all . . ."

She knew exactly what *it* meant, and *it* made her seethe even more.

"Well then, I might be able to take a second look. But you're going to have to give me a little more incentive than just a bill that works for *you*." He sucked his teeth.

Rose had never crossed ethical lines in all of her years as a lobbyist. She was too good at what she did to need to bribe someone. She would get them on her team because she was just that smart—not because new lobbyist legislation had been passed. She didn't need to pay them or sleep with them, even though she'd had multiple requests for both. But those things were against her moral code, even if other ethical lines were becoming suspect. In fact, Rose was known in a town of little ethics for a strong stance in hers; that's why she found Senator Tomason's request so loathsome and why it made her so angry. But she had never had a bill this important. This high-profile. The president had even been talking about it. And about her, so she had heard.

She couldn't believe her next words. "We'll take another look at it. I'll call you later with my response. But for the record, I find this proposal from someone of your stature very offensive. You knew I was away, and to try to slip this one by me really isn't something I thought you would stoop to, Senator."

He chuckled that fake laugh. "I shock even myself sometimes, Rose."

They hung up with multiple opportunities hanging in the air. Rose spent the next hour mentally processing their conversation. And making herself sick that she was even contemplating his insulting suggestion. But she had shocked herself with her actions quite a bit lately. What was one more area of weakness?

———～———

Rose tried the radio again to drown out her thoughts, but the jazz station had turned to static. She scanned the channels for other offerings. The light-pop station filled Rose's car with the familiar sounds of Corey Hart's "Sunglasses at Night." She couldn't help but laugh to herself, thinking of how she used to dance around the house with her sunglasses on to the sounds of this song.

She sang along, surprising herself that she remembered every word. A U-Haul moving van drove up beside her. As it passed, the young man in the passenger's seat eyed her curiously. Her face flushed with embarrassment. She watched as the van continued by her, remembering the last time she had seen those orange letters. That move had changed her life. It changed the lives of her entire family.

———⌣———

Rosey and Christopher heard "We're moving to Myrtle Beach" one evening just before bedtime. They hated the words before the sentence was even finished.

Eleven and fourteen weren't the ages when kids wanted to change their lives. "You've got to be kidding me!" Rosey felt the horror settle in. "We can't leave Mamaw and Granddaddy! And I can't leave Jenny! There's no way you can do this to us!"

But they did. Rosey's father had taken a job leading praise and worship at another church, a larger church. It was what he felt *led* to do.

Rosey's mother took her into her arms and held her. They cried together. After all, Rosey's mother had never lived any-where except with her parents or down the street from her parents in her thirty-five years of living.

But one month later the U-Haul was packed and headed for Myrtle Beach. A move that Rosey was certain her father had come to regret. And one that Rosey's mother had allowed to destroy their family.

———⌣———

Outside of the suburbs, the Virginia hills clearly stated how peaceful life could actually be. Even the air here felt different from DC. She had been on the road for two hours, and it only took a couple of hours for Rose to get hungry. She pulled off the interstate somewhere near Richmond and scanned each side of the street slowly, only to realize there wasn't a restaurant or recognizable gas station to be found.

"I am a genius," she said aloud, scolding her inability to observe exit signs before actually taking one.

A small gas station had a large neon sign with a blinking arrow in front of its store. The station looked like something from a country music video. But it was the black lettering on the sign that got her attention: "Boiled Peanuts." Rose hadn't had boiled peanuts in years.

A wiry old man approached in used-up denim overalls, pulling the sides of his flannel cap down over his ears. She cracked the window. "Hello, little lady," he said, touching the bill. "Can I get you a fill-up?" His name patch confirmed that he was Herschel. And she had no idea why he wasn't wearing a coat in this frigid weather.

She studied her surroundings. The cold air and the smell of gas flooded her senses. So full-service stations still existed? She had no idea. The last full-service station she'd seen was the one she and Christopher used to pull into every other morning on the way to school. He'd get two dollars' worth of gas from the self-serve pump. And then they would enjoy the rest of the trip to school singing "Islands in the Stream." For some reason that song came on the radio almost every morning.

And now, somewhere in the vicinity of Richmond, Virginia, she eyed her gas gauge. Still a good three hours or more on that tank, but the sharpness in the wind didn't offer any great appeal to stop later and fill it up herself.

"Well, if you could just top it off, that would be great," she answered. As she emerged from the car, she grabbed her wrap and closed the door. She hurried past Herschel and into the shelter, obviously an old house later christened a gas station.

After a few moments of browsing, she spotted a big, heated metal container of peanuts in the middle of the store. The handle of the ladle protruded from the side. She frowned. She liked her peanuts cold.

The cowbell that hung around the handle of the glass door rang. She was pretty sure it was Herschel by the shuffle of his boots against the concrete floor.

"Are these the only kind of boiled peanuts you have?" she asked without turning around.

"Oh no. We've got some back here in the cooler. That's the way I like 'em." Maybe some wouldn't have understood his strong dialect, but Rose did. Just because she didn't speak Southern anymore didn't mean she'd lost her ability to under-stand it. She watched his feeble-looking black hand grasp the cooler door with more strength than she expected. With his Sammy Davis Jr. build, she wasn't quite sure how he opened it so readily.

She saw the little brown bag and couldn't help but smile. There, sitting in front of her, was a sack of boiled peanuts just the way she liked them. This was exactly the way her dad always bought them for her at Cromer's whenever they traveled to Columbia. Cromer's slogan was "Guaranteed the Worst in Town." People knew better. They came like old people to Bingo night.

"Thank you so much," she said, refraining from snatching them from the poor man's hand.

"But you can't eat cold boiled peanuts without a little something to go with it," he said, motioning his index finger for Rose to follow. He slowly led her down one of the aisles that held all the food Rose had called cursed years ago. The Doritos, the Twinkies, the Sugar Babies. She tried to conceal her amusement.

"You headed somewhere special?" he asked as he scooted.

"I'm headed to my mamaw's," she responded, not sure why she told him the truth. Because in the South, the truth always took too long. Especially hers.

He stopped at the toiletry rack and turned around. "She'll be tickled to death to see you, I'm sure." He grinned, revealing a glimmering section of gold teeth.

She pondered his statement. "I hope so," she replied. "I hope so."

He resumed their trek and rounded the corner, and she caught sight of their destination. Situated up against the wall was an old Coca-Cola dispenser. Rose couldn't remember the last time she'd had a drink from a glass Coca-Cola bottle. She leaned against the rack next to her.

"They don't come any better than this, little lady," he said, reaching inside and pulling one out. "But I keep it a little colder than most. I betcha it'll be just like you like it." He winked. Then with one flick of the wrist, he had the bottle cap off and falling to the bottom of the opener that was attached to the Coke dispenser.

The rush of the cold wind and the ringing of the cowbell on the door caught the old man's attention. "You enjoy that Coca-Cola, little lady. I'll be right back." He went to help the new customer.

Rose nodded absently. She watched as the warmth of her hand melted the frost on the bottle.

———~———

"You got me again, Granddaddy!" Rosey squealed, pointing at the checkerboard. Granddaddy smiled at her. He sat in his green iron chair with the white lattice. The chair had been there for at least as long as Rosey had been around. "Let's play again . . . just one more time, Granddaddy! I can win if you give me one more time."

"All right, Red, one more time. But you be careful, baby girl, because I'm ready for you." Granddaddy had called her Red from the day her mama and daddy brought her home from the hospital—already with hair as auburn as a sunset. At least that's what Granddaddy told her.

They played a few minutes in silence. Rosey concentrated on her winning strategy.

Granddaddy's old hound, Scout, got up to survey whatever Christopher and Bobby Dean were busy doing on the other side of the porch. The dog bumped Rosey, who bumped the small television tray they played on, but her granddaddy steadied it just in time. Just in time, that is, for Rosey's final move. She planted her red checker firmly.

"I gotcha, Granddaddy! I gotcha!" She stood up and did a victory dance.

He chuckled. "I do believe you got me, Red. I do believe you got me."

Mamaw's head peeked out of the house. "Rosey, Mamaw's got something for you she thinks you're going to like," she coaxed.

Rosey's eyes grew wide when she saw Mamaw's apron on. That meant Rosey was going to get something from the kitchen. Rosey loved Mamaw's kitchen. In fact, Rosey thought, if it hadn't been for Mamaw's cooking, their entire family probably would've starved by now. Because Rosey's mother couldn't cook anything. Made it hard to believe that Mamaw was even her mother's mama, come to think of it. Rosey figured maybe her mother had been adopted.

Rosey ran inside and paid no attention as the screen door slapped shut behind her. She smelled fried chicken. There was no smell she loved more. In the kitchen, Mamaw's upper half, including her ample bosom, was hidden by the freezer door. All Rosey could see was her bottom half—round stomach covered by her blue floral dress, and skinny calves sticking out from the hem. An edge of her green apron also showed. Mamaw, white hair in a neat bun on the back of her head, finally emerged holding two bottles.

"What is it, Mamaw?" Rosey asked, craning her neck and squinting her eyes to see. After all, with Mamaw, you were usually getting a national treasure. At least her fried chicken should be declared one.

Mamaw closed the freezer door and smiled at her. "It's a soda, baby girl." She placed one in Rosey's tiny hand.

Rosey stared at it. She loved sodas. She'd have lived on sodas if her parents would have let her. They didn't. But she'd never seen a soda like this before. It was a glass Coke bottle, all icy and cold. In fact, it was freezing her hand. "What did you do to it?"

"I put it in the freezer," Mamaw said, turning to rummage through one of the kitchen drawers. She pulled out a bottle opener and turned back to Rosey. "Now watch this."

There wasn't any sense in Mamaw's words, because Rosey hadn't taken her eyes off that bottle since it came out of the freezer. Her hand was completely numb, but she didn't care. Her mamaw wrapped her hand around Rosey's and flipped off the cap. Rosey watched as the frost inched down the bottle.

"Try it," Mamaw prodded.

"It's so cold!" Rosey giggled. But then she took a long swig. Her eyes widened as she drank long and hard. She came up for air with a gasp, her eyes watering.

Mamaw's belly shook. "It's not going anywhere. Here, take Granddaddy one to enjoy with you."

Rosey took the other bottle from Mamaw's hands and headed back to the door. There she stopped and turned around. "Mamaw, can you make me another one of these for later? Because I'm already feeling like I'll be pretty thirsty around three o'clock."

"Three o'clock, huh?" Mamaw's belly shook harder.

"Yeah, three o'clock. I'm sure that's when I'll need me another one." The screen door tapped closed behind her.

———~———

When the whoosh of cold air hit Rosey again, she realized she'd been standing there like an idiot. She hurried up to the counter and handed Herschel her credit card to pay for the gas. He handed her back her card and nodded toward the goodies in her hand.

"So those'll be one dollar," Herschel said, holding out his hand.

A moment went by before his demand registered. "Only a dollar? Surely these cost more than a dollar?"

"Nope. Today's special is one dollar for all ladies travelin' to see their mamaws." He raised one of his bushy eyebrows, and his grin offered her the confirmation that she would probably be one of many getting the Herschel treatment today. He winked again. He probably made everyone feel special.

"Then I picked the perfect place for a snack, huh?" She smiled and winked back.

She laid one crisp dollar bill in Herschel's hand. Before she could withdraw her hand, he wrapped his fingers around it. Startled, she lifted her eyes to meet his own, coal black and gazing at her deeply. "It's nice every now and then to find yourself a reminder of home. But I bet getting home will be even nicer."

He didn't know her home.

"And I hope when you get there, you find it better than you left it." He gave her one more gold-illuminated smile and released her. A chill ran through her. She didn't look back as she walked out the door and back to her car.

After she nestled herself into the plush leather, she eyed her bottle once more. She brought it to her lips with near reverence and drank long and hard. By the time she pulled it from her lips, her eyes and her throat were burning.

She'd almost forgotten what it tasted like. But odd how when lost things returned, remembering why you loved them in the first place didn't take long.

She moved her gaze to the little paper bag. It had been so long. And you couldn't find boiled peanuts in her neck of the woods. She pulled one out and cracked it open with her teeth. The pleasure came back to her immediately. She removed half of the shell and placed the other side full of peanuts and salty juice into her mouth. She sucked on those peanuts long and determined. They were perfect.

She cracked another one open, pulled out a large peanut, and examined it. The size was similar to the fat piece of crayon she had lodged up her nose when she was four. She had simply wanted to see if the crayon would fit. Thank the good Lord it didn't. But it did squeeze in there just far enough that neither her mama nor her daddy could get it out without help. She considered for a moment the wonderment that led a child to see if a fat crayon would fit up her nose. Rose looked around to make sure no one was watching her. Then she studied the peanut again, wondering. And then she laughed. No one heard her. But she heard herself. And that was enough.

She sat there in her car, enjoying each salty and juicy peanut, until she finished the entire bag and her entire Coca-Cola, all while the little red light blinked on the top of her BlackBerry.

Inside the store, Herschel took a dollar rose from the vase beside the register. He laid down the single bill the stranger had handed him next to the vase. The roses had been delivered yesterday by the sweet lady who owned the flower shop a quarter mile up the road. They were beginning to open. He picked up one that seemed to be the largest among them, a red one looking powerful and proud. He brought it to his nose and inhaled deeply of its fragrance. Then he cut off the stem and tucked the rosebud inside the pocket in the front of his overalls. The pocket hung slightly with the weight and covered up the *H* of his name. But he didn't mind going through the rest of the day as "erschel." No, not today. Because there was something about that little lady who had just passed through that made him feel she might need some praying-for today. And for some reason he felt this flower wouldn't let him forget to do just that.

4

"Did you get it?"

Rose turned on her blinker to pass the slow-moving car in the fast-moving lane. "Get what?"

"You did not just say, 'Get what,'" Helen responded in bewildered amusement. "Rose, did you get the document I sent you?"

Had poor Rose still been eating peanuts, one would have lodged itself in her nose all by itself. She became suddenly aware of the BlackBerry in the small pocket inside her door. It looked as if it were smoldering. Rose didn't forget e-mails. Rose didn't forget anything. "I haven't had time to pull over yet," she lied. Lying had become easier the more she did it. It seemed to be increasing in frequency.

"Oh, well, thank goodness. Because I thought you had

forgotten, and if you forgot to check your e-mail, then I might as well quit and move in with my sister. Because neither you nor I can keep our jobs if you've become bipolar. Of course, my sister wants to set me up with a preacher. So maybe that isn't such a good idea."

"For you or the preacher?"

"Funny, but don't change the subject."

Rose laughed that spit kind of laugh, the one where the sound comes out through your teeth, like *Phhhh*. "I didn't forget," she said. "Just trying to make good time. And if these slow people would quit driving in the fast lane, I might actually get somewhere."

"Now, that's the Rose I know. Focused. Diligent. And irritable." Helen said the words as if they were simply the truth to be told. "So call me when you get it, and we can figure out what I need to have prepared for your meeting. By the way, what color do you think I should paint my nails next week? Did you see that new shade of red in *In Style* that cute Reese Witherspoon wore to that hoity-toity awards show?"

"I do not care what color you paint your nails, Helen."

"Like I said, an irritable little creature you are."

Rose cut off the phone with no good-bye. People defined Rose all the time. Behind her back. To her face. On the streets of Washington. Even on the *Hannity and Colmes* show the other night, so she heard. People didn't care. Everyone had an impression of her. But was she really irritable? I mean, focused and diligent, sure. Even tenacious, maybe. But irritable? She wasn't sure she liked irritable. In fact, she wasn't quite sure when irritable arrived. Of course, that's how it usually happens when something has been your companion for awhile. You have absolutely no idea how long it's been there or when exactly it showed up.

———◡———

"Don't be a whiny butt, Charlotte," Bobby Dean said, bopping his sister on the top of the head.

Bobby Dean and Charlotte were blocking Rosey's view, and who knew just when they might start tussling for real. She scooted over on the couch to get out of the way.

"Mamaaaw . . ." Charlotte whined, throwing her hand on her hip in perfect Southern drama. "Bobby Dean called me a whiny rutt . . ."

"No, I called you a whiny *butt*," he corrected.

His interjection stopped her whining. Momentarily. "Mamaaaw . . . he called me a whiny butt," she said, stomping into the kitchen.

Mamaw called from the kitchen. "Bobby Dean, we'll have none of that, now, you hear?"

"But she's always so irritable. Can't you make her not be so irritable?"

"Charlotte," Mamaw responded, "you need to quit being a tattletale and stop ruining a perfectly good Saturday morning."

Charlotte could ruin a perfectly good anything with one of her tantrums. And she had just about ruined their cartoon. This one had Scooby wrapped around Shaggy as if they were Siamese twins while a ghost hovered over their heads. Rosey and Christopher shared a pillow. He was still in his Superman pj's, and she was still wearing her Cinderella nightgown. Bobby Dean didn't like pajamas, so he was running around in his Underoos.

The smell of fresh-baked cookies wafted into the family room. Of course, it wasn't that far for the aroma to travel in Mamaw and Granddaddy's twelve-hundred-square-foot, five-room house. With only two bedrooms, one bathroom, a family room, and a kitchen, it was small and cozy. But it felt like a mansion to Rosey.

Her mamaw and granddaddy had been born and raised in Mullins. And Rosey's family lived within spittin' distance. Mamaw often said that life couldn't get any better. They had their own baby girl and son-in-law close by, and their grand-babies were "the center of their universe." That meant Rosey. *And* Charlotte.

Granddaddy had worked tobacco fields all of his life. And Mamaw had cooked three meals a day for him and his crew, until he decided to retire. Now she cooked only for her own crew. Rosey later figured that nobody else bothered to cook because no matter what they made, it wasn't as good as Mamaw's cooking.

"Who wants to lick the spoon?" Mamaw called from the kitchen. She was standing in front of the table that sat in the center of the room. The cookies were supposed to be their treat after lunch. But Mamaw had trouble waiting for such things.

They were all takers. Charlotte, however, was perched atop the table, already working on her spoon. "I need some more, Mamaw," she said, cramming the full spoon into her mouth.

"You will wait until everyone else has some." Rosey loved Mamaw. She gave each of them a whopping spoonful of flour, sugar, eggs, and milk. Each time they ate a heap of that raw dough, they risked getting worms—at least that's what Rosey's mama told her eating raw dough would do to you, but apparently Mamaw didn't worry much about their getting worms. So why should Rosey worry?

Mamaw had enough spoons for everyone. Even Charlotte got a little more. As irritating as she was.

The day passed with only one bloody nose, three Charlotte tantrums, and one bruising game of tag. By nightfall Rosey had convinced her daddy to let her spend the night at her mamaw and granddaddy's—again. Everyone else headed back to their own homes.

After Mamaw tucked Rosey into bed, she heard Mamaw pad back into the family room. She knew the creaking of Mamaw's knees meant that she was kneeling beside her recliner.

Rosey got up and sneaked over to the door that Mamaw always left cracked for her so she could get some light streaming into her room from the kitchen. She listened as Mamaw named each one of her nine children and their spouses and all her thousands of grandchildren by name. Rosey thought it was a miracle that Mamaw could remember all those names.

And at the end of Mamaw's list, just when she thought Mamaw might have actually forgotten the grandchild sleeping in her own house, she heard Mamaw add, "And, dear Jesus, bless our little Rose. She's such a sweet girl. Please don't ever let that sweetness be taken from her."

Rosey slipped back into bed. Nestling her face against her pillow, which smelled like Mamaw's rose water, she fell fast asleep.

Irritable. The mere thought of the word made her irritable. "I'm not irritable," she assured the silence in the car. "Charlotte was the irritable one. Always whining and getting her way. I always did everything right." She stopped herself there. She had lied enough.

Anyway, she wasn't irritable. She was just easily frustrated. "Yeah . . ."

No, that wasn't good either. Okay, here it was: she had high expectations, and not everyone was willing to meet them, because not everyone was as tenacious as she was. Yeah. That was it. She was certain that was it.

She drove in silence until she could no longer stand the

incessant noise of her own thoughts. She clicked on the radio and began to flip through the stations.

"Our soloist who will be initiating the chant is Nellie Ryanockov. We will give the interpretation."

Rose pressed the search button. "No chants today. It's Thursday. I'm absolutely certain this is my no-chant day."

"Great is thy faithfulness . . . Great is thy faithfulness."

"No more religion today. Helen's mention of a preacher was enough," she said, pressing the button. She was feeling irritated.

"Tequila makes her clothes fall off," the country singer crooned.

"Now, that's visual," she said, laughing to herself, the irritability lifting as suddenly as it had come. She listened for awhile, tapped the steering wheel a time or two, then hit the search button just as the song closed with whooping and hollering.

"I can't fight this feeling any longer."

Rose felt her breath slip away. She hadn't heard that song in years. A lot of years. All the way back to Billy Monroe years. Now, *that* was a place she hadn't traveled in, well, years.

———

"Have you met your pastor's brother-in-law?" Rosey's best friend, Jenny, asked her one day as they were walking back up to Jenny's house from Mamaw's.

The Church of God that Rosey and her family attended

was right next door to Mamaw and Granddaddy's. In fact, they pretty much shared a parking lot with each other. And apparently seeing the church had caused Jenny to remember the new arrival in town.

"What's a brother-in-law, exactly?" Rosey inquired, swiveling to look at Jenny.

"It's Pastor Coleman's wife's brother." The mouthful came out surprisingly clear. "He's here visiting from Florence for awhile."

"How do *you* know what a brother-in-law is?"

"You know," said Jenny, her little mind processing, "I have no idea how I know what a brother-in-law is. I guess I've just heard my mama talk about it."

"Well, how does your mama know all of this? Y'all don't even go to our church."

They'd stopped at this point and were staring at Rosey's church.

Jenny's family went to the AME church three streets over. She was the chocolate to Rosey's strawberry and Charlotte's vanilla. Together they all three made up the perfect napoleon ice cream! At least that's what they called it.

"We live on the same street. What do you expect?" Apparently same-street dwelling brought extra information. "Plus, my mama knows everything about everybody else's mama. Probably knows things about your mama that your daddy doesn't even know."

Rosey examined Jenny's face to see if she was as serious as she sounded. Because there was no way someone knew more about her mama than her daddy. No way at all. "What's he look like? The brother-in-law guy?"

A glint of mischief appeared in Jenny's eyes. "I think I saw him go in the church when I was headed down to your mamaw's."

"Who? My dad?"

She slapped Rosey. "No, silly, the brother-in-law guy."

She had Rosey going good now. "Oh, really?"

"You wanna sneak around back and see if we can see him?" She giggled, covering her mouth as if giggling might undo her suggestion.

Rosey's gaze met Jenny's at the same time. Without any more words they snatched each other's hand and headed to the back door of the church.

"What if someone finds us?" Rosey asked, trying to catch her breath.

Jenny's small hand reached for the door handle. "If they catch us, I'll just let them know that you've been sinning again and we needed to get you saved before Sunday. You know, so you can come to church and all."

Sounded good enough to Rosey. The door creaked as they opened it. Rosey snickered, and Jenny nudged her. "Shh." Then the brightly colored baubles that held Jenny's braided pigtails kept knocking into each other. The sound was so loud that Rosey finally grabbed her pigtails and held them together to prevent all the clanging. But it was about then that they heard clanging of another kind coming from the front of the church.

"What's that?" Rosey whispered.

Jenny didn't seem to hear her. "Let's sneak into the pool."

"You mean where they dunk people?"

"Yeah, the baptist pool. Let's sneak in there and see what's making all that racket."

The baptismal pool still had a few water remnants from Sunday's baptism of a family of four. Rosey and Jenny perched themselves on the top step and peered over the small acrylic divider that prevented the water from splashing the choir.

What eleven-year-old Rosey saw was about to change her world. She saw the back of the brother-in-law's long, sun-streaked tresses. They bounced with each beat of the bass drum, and when he went to hit the snare, she could see his profile of perfection. Now, to anyone else, Billy Monroe might've looked like a lanky fourteen-year-old. But to Rosey and Jenny, he looked like a dream.

They stayed squatted on the top step of the baptistery until their legs fell asleep. And when they finally got their legs to working again and left the church that day, Rosey knew that Billy Monroe was the man she would marry. And had it not been for the kiss that never happened and Rosey's interaction with a bird, it just might have come to be.

Billy and Rosey caught each other's eyes the next Sunday at church. Rosey always sat on the second maroon velvet–cushioned pew next to her mamaw and granddaddy, while her mother played the church piano and her daddy led the choir. Her entire family was musical. Even Christopher. But Rosey couldn't carry a tune in a bucket. And Christopher reminded her every time she tried.

He would say, "Mama, don't let Rosey sing. One day someone is actually going to hear her, and she's going to embarrass us all."

But Billy didn't seem bothered about Rosey's lack of musical talent. Or perhaps he couldn't hear her sing from across the aisle. Instead, he seemed interested in Rosey's other abilities.

On her way out of church, Rosey heard his voice. "Want to meet me down by the river after lunch?" Billy asked through smacking rubber bands that were attached to his double layer of braces.

Rosey stopped on the bricked bottom step of the church and tried to look at him. She didn't care that he hadn't so much as introduced himself.

"You can bring Jenny if you want," he offered.

Obviously Jenny or Jenny's mama had already introduced the two of them.

"Um, yeah . . ." She fiddled with the edges of her cape, which matched the trim of her dress. For some reason at this moment, she was feeling a tad juvenile in the ensemble. "I'll see you there later."

"Yeah, well, later then." And off he went lankily. Hands in pockets. Braces causing his lips to protrude, and shoes scuffing the sidewalk. He was perfect.

Rosey had to wait for another hour to call Jenny, because Jenny's church ran a bit longer than the Church of God. And if the Spirit got to moving down there, well, you could kiss Jenny good-bye until time for Sunday night church. Because the women in the white dresses and white hats would snatch a child by her pigtails and wedge her back in her seat before they let the moving of the Spirit be interrupted. Rosey knew because Jenny had endured multiple retractions.

When Rosey finally got through to Jenny, she whispered into the receiver, "Hurry up and eat so you can go with me to the river." Rosey had stretched the small curly cord all the way into her closet. She pulled a pair of jeans in front of her face to try to muffle her sounds even more. "You don't have to stay, but I have to be able to tell Mama and Daddy that we're going together."

"Are you going down there to see Billy?" She knew Jenny was probably hopping with excitement. Had Rosey been with her, she would have jerked her to a stop.

"Yes, but we can't let anyone know. My parents will kill

me. Plus, we have to act mature. He is fourteen, you know," Rosey said, clearing her throat.

Jenny stopped hopping. Rosey could tell by the more dignified tone. "Yes, you're right. We must show our maturation. So call me when you're ready to head that way."

"I *am* calling you. That means I'm already ready to head that way, so hurry! Get in there and eat whatever it is y'all are eating, and meet me outside. I'll be waiting at the corner."

"You can be so demanding," Jenny huffed. "Are you wearing your suit?"

"My bathing suit?" Rosey responded, making it clear it had never crossed her mind. "No way. I'm not wearing my bathing suit."

"Well, we *are* going to the river," Jenny reminded.

"I don't care. I'm still not letting him see me in my bathing suit. I'll just swim in my shorts if I need to."

That wasn't enough for Jenny. "Won't that look suspicious? Us going to the river in our clothes?"

"You don't always have to swim at the river," Rosey retorted.

"You don't?"

"No, sometimes people just walk by the river, throw rocks in the river, sit by the river. Only children have to always swim in the river."

"Oh . . ." Jenny said slowly. "I see. This is all about the maturation thing."

"Yes, my sweet, silly Jenny—this is all about our maturation."

5

A new song propelled Rose back to reality. She and Jenny hadn't talked in years. Not since Rose's life blew up and she went to college. Last she heard, Jenny had married a former professional football player turned pastor and was living somewhere in Nashville. Come to think of it, Jenny had actually called her a few times in past years, but for some reason Rose never called her back. In fact, until this moment she hadn't thought about Jenny in ages.

Rose raced by a smoldering car with a child in the backseat. She slowed and caught a glimpse in her rearview mirror of a frantic woman emerging from the well-worn vehicle with smoke billowing from the hood. Rose didn't stop for strangers. Where she came from, they would rob you or even kill you. But her car braked and pulled onto the shoulder.

"I've gone over the deep end today," she assured herself.

It was certain. This was the only explanation for why in the world she had just pulled over to help a complete stranger. She moved the sleek gearshift into reverse and rolled backward, but she stopped a few yards from the billowing smoke. If the car blew, she didn't want the explosion messing up her car in the process.

Rose's two-inch-heeled boots clicked on the pavement as she headed toward the clearly upset traveler. She wrapped her shawl tightly around her shoulders to defend against the bitter cold. Granted, a sweat suit would have been more appropriate attire for the journey. But not for Rose. No, her baby blue cashmere sweater and perfectly flowing chocolate wool pants were how Rose traveled. To Rose all details mattered. Because everything in her life said something.

Rose raised her hand to shield some of the wind from her face as it whipped her hair. "Can I help you, ma'am?"

The frazzled face looked up at her in desperation. "I don't know what to do!" The woman paced in front of the car with her hands jammed in her coat pockets, shivering. "I told my husband it was going to break down, but he wouldn't believe me! My little boy is back there, and it's cold, and—ooh, I could just scream!"

"It's okay. It's going to be okay," Rose said, reaching out her hands, hoping to stay the woman's nerves. "Have you called him yet?"

The woman squinted at Rose. "Lady, do you see a pay phone around here anywhere?"

Rose had forgotten pay phones existed. "How about I just let you use my cell phone, and we'll call somebody to come get you."

"You'd do that for me?" The woman's eyes softened, glistening through her frustrated tears.

"Sure, just bring your little boy to my car, and you both can stay warm while you make your call."

The tears dried up instantly, and the woman scanned Rose up and down as if making sure Rose wasn't some stranger coming to kill her. That caused Rose to chuckle inside, relieving the murder worries of her own. "You aren't some crazy murderer in expensive clothes, are you?"

Well, honesty was good. And rather welcome in a moment like this. Rose smiled. "No, I assure you. I have no murdering agenda today." Maybe that wasn't the best phrase.

"What do you mean *today*? Have you had one some other day?" The woman moved to the side of the car.

Rose reached her hands out again. "No, no, I was just joking. In fact, I was wondering if I should even pick you up, in case *you* were some kind of murderer. So I guess that means we're both pretty safe."

"That's my treasure back there," the lady said, pointing to the sleeping child in the car seat in the back. "I can't let anything happen to him."

"Then let's get him into a warm car and get somebody to take you home." She motioned.

The stranded motorist gave Rose the once-over one more time, but she eventually made up her mind and walked to the back of the car, unlocked the car seat, and picked up the diaper bag. She refused to let Rose carry any of her belongings, so all Rose could do was watch the stranger lug them and her child to her car. Even with all the commotion, including the clicking of the seat belt into the new backseat, the towheaded baby never opened his eyes.

Once they were settled in the car, Rose pulled off her wrap and laid it in her lap. She handed the phone to the woman.

"I'll try my husband first," she said, studying Rose's Black-Berry. "How's this fandangled thing work?" She blew at a piece of hair that had come loose from her neatly clasped ponytail.

"Here, let me help you." Rose dialed the number and watched as the stranger placed it up against her ear, then pulled it back just to make sure it was working, then put it back against her head one more time.

Rose started the car and turned up the heat. She turned the seat heaters on, but she didn't bother explaining that one.

"Hello? Hello?" the lady said into the receiver. "Is Walter there? . . . He's what? At lunch?" She looked at her watch. "Well, tell him I'm stranded on the side of the road, and he needs to come and get me, because it's all his fault anyway!" she announced.

Rose thought she was the only one who talked into phones that way. This was irritable. Rose wasn't irritable. This lady was irritable. Of course, she *was* stranded by the side of the road in freezing-cold weather, with a baby in the backseat, but if Helen had heard this woman, then she would know that Rose wasn't the only one who had irritability issues.

Her passenger laughed. "And then tell him we're all fine and that we love him. Because if you don't tell him that, he'll worry himself into a case of irritable bowel syndrome, and I don't have time for that today either."

Apparently irritability ran in the family.

"How do you cut this thing off?" she asked, holding out the BlackBerry as if it might come to life.

Rose took it, noting the woman's soft and clean hands as she did. She looked in her rearview mirror and studied the little boy's face. Clean and sweet. The car seat was older, she could tell, but even though their clothes looked as worn as their vehicle, their appearance was neat and tidy. Rose wasn't sure what she had expected. Ketchup stains maybe.

"I'm Lilly," the now-identified stranger said as she darted her hand into Rose's driving area.

Rose scrunched up her arm since her hand didn't have far to travel to greet the welcoming appendage. "I'm Rose. Rose Fletcher."

"Well, we could just open us up a greenhouse," Lilly said, cracking herself up.

Rose gazed at her companion and couldn't help but smile. "You know," she said, "I could just take you home, if you don't mind leaving your car here."

Lilly's animated expression grew solemn.

"But I don't have to, if you don't want me to." Rose added quickly, trying to squelch another case of nerves.

"No, no . . ." Lilly paused. "You'd do that? I mean, you've just been so nice already. I couldn't ask you to do any more."

Rose glanced at the clock. At the rate she was going, she wouldn't see home until midnight. Surely the time to take Lilly home was less than the time she would use up sitting here in the hope that Walter chose a short lunch and didn't work too far away. "Really, it's no bother."

"Well, I only live about ten minutes up the road. I'd walk it if it weren't so cold," she said, turning her head to gaze out the window. Except for the evergreens that lined the inter-state and separated them from the access road, the trees were barren.

"No, no one's walking in this. You just give me directions and I'll get you and your little fella home," Rose said, putting the car in drive and pulling onto the highway. "What's his name?"

"That's Walter Wally Williams the third." She giggled and put her hand over her mouth. "Isn't that pitiful? That a child would go through his entire life being called Walter Wally Williams the third. So I just call him Jack," she said with a shrug of her shoulders. As if that were a completely logical substitute.

"I told my Walter, one Walter around here is enough. So we're calling our boy Jack."

The mention of her husband's name caused Rose to shift in her seat. "Well, I think Jack is a fine name." That was the best she could muster.

"Well, he's the pride of our life," Lilly said and turned in her seat for a moment to admire her little fella. "It took me and Walter ten years to get all the plumbing working, if you know what I mean. We thought about everything though. In vitro. Out vitro." She chuckled. "A surrogate. A neighbor. My word, we were about ready to see if my mama could have him for us."

Rose hoped the horror on her face was erased before Lilly saw it.

"That was exactly how I felt." Obviously Lilly didn't miss much. "So Walter and I finally told the Lord, 'Lord, we're not sure why you haven't given us any children. But the thought of our mama carrying one for us just feels a little, well, weird. So if we end up having to adopt, you know what we need. All babies need a home.' And it wasn't three months later I was throwing up lunch, and I had never been so happy in all my life. Six months later, Jack made his appearance."

Rose looked back at the little guy. She couldn't believe that he hadn't so much as stirred. The ache pressed forward. Her mind pushed it back. And she focused back on the road.

"So what about you?" asked Lilly. "Any little Jacks float-ing around? I notice that you don't have a wedding ring on, but nowadays that doesn't mean you don't have a baby or two."

Now would've been a perfect time for little Jack to rise and shine. Rose stared at her hand on the steering wheel. There was still a slight white tan line from either the summer or the ten years that had left a permanent remnant of her and Jack's life. Unfortunately, Rose was still trying to erase any other remnants. "Little Jacks?" she managed.

"Yeah, rugrats, mongrels, precious littles."

Rose's grip on the steering wheel tightened. So did the pressure on her chest. "No. No little Jacks floating around. No little Jacks at all . . ." Her voice quieted.

"Well, it's probably best, honey. If you don't have a hus-band, you really don't need to try to raise one on your own. They can be demanding little critters. Don't let that angelic face back there fool you." She laughed again. "Actually, you may as well. He's one of the most perfect little people I've ever been around."

Rose had wanted perfect. Strived for perfection. Un-fortunately for Rose, perfection came with too great a price.

———

Jack placed the small package beside Rose's dinner plate. They were using the Lynn Chase Jaguar Jungle pattern they had registered for when they married five years earlier. The first few years of their marriage had been wonderful. For those years they had just enjoyed life together. Especially buying and renovating their home. The Cape Cod was a disaster when they bought it. The washer and dryer were in the master bathroom. They thought that would make for great conversation but moved them to the second floor anyway. They took out walls, mirrored others, and wallpapered more. And by the time they were through, they loved it and each other more.

Those first few years, there wasn't a room that love couldn't be made in. But Rose noticed a tear in the sofa about the time the tears in the marriage appeared. And the enjoyment had turned more businesslike, formal, different.

The teriyaki-glazed salmon with saffron rice on their plates was like something out of a magazine. But all Rose's meals were. Beautiful. Pristine. Perfect. Just like Rose's appearance. Just like their house. And Rose made each and every meal all by herself.

"What's this?" Rose asked when she saw the beautifully wrapped present. She sat down, picked up her linen napkin, and laid it neatly across her lap.

Jack tucked her chair in. "It's for you, beautiful," he said, kissing the top of her head, then seating himself.

She picked up the delicate white box and untied the pink ribbon. She laid the ribbon neatly by her plate and lifted the small lid. She moved the tissue that covered the treasure, and when she caught a glimpse of what was inside, she felt a sudden streak of fear cascade through her entire body.

Jack studied her. It wasn't something they hadn't talked about. It just wasn't something they had talked about lately. "You know what it is, don't you?" he asked.

Rose collected herself. "Sure, yes, sure I do. It's that baby rattle you've had since you were little."

"Yeah, it's the one you wanted to make sure we saved for our baby. Well, I think it's about time for that baby, don't you?" he asked softly.

Rose laid the box next to her plate without pulling out the silver-plated baby rattle.

"We've been married five years. Aren't you ready to start a family?" She saw fear creep into Jack's eyes.

"It's just . . ." She searched every cavity of her mind for some viable reason. Or at least a reason he'd believe.

"I know," he said, clearly trying to reassure her. "I know, it doesn't feel like the right time with your career going as well as it is, and with the way I still have to travel. But now that you're getting busier at work, then maybe we could take some pressure off of you here. Hire a housekeeper maybe. Eat out some and not feel like you have to make dinner every night. That's a lot of pressure, Rosey. And I don't expect you to do everything."

Rose squirmed in her seat. "But I can't quit my job and raise children. Is that what you want from me? No, my job is too important right now, and these are defining years for me."

Jack got up out of his chair and walked over to hers. He knelt at her side, very similar to the way he had six years earlier when he had asked her to marry him. She saw the hurt in his face.

"I know you love your job. And you're great at your job." He took her hands from her lap and brought them to his mouth. He kissed them softly, and his hazel eyes made their way back to her face. "I don't want to take anything from you. I'm just trying to help you realize that not everything has to be perfect around here for us to have children. The house doesn't have to be perfect, baby. Shoot, if we want to leave our underwear on the bathroom floor or not make the bed for a day, it's not going to kill us, I promise."

She wasn't convinced.

"I want part of me and you together. I want a piece of us in this world. I want to see someone with your beautiful eyes and my charming personality."

She took her hand and rubbed his face softly. She truly loved him. But she wasn't sure she loved him this much. "I'll try," she finally offered.

"You will?" His face lit up.

"But it could take awhile," she reminded. "Babies aren't made the first time you try."

"That's all right," he said, pulling her out of her chair. "I'll enjoy the trying." He kissed her softly. And in a few moments, Rose and Jack were reliving the passion that had been theirs in those first few years together. And the salmon and saffron rice were just heated up later.

Once Jack had fallen asleep, Rose crawled out of bed and went into the bathroom. She quietly removed the birth control pills from the trash can where Jack and she had earlier thrown them away together. She hid them in a purse in the closet. They'd be safe there.

She leaned against the edge of the closet door and was unable to prevent the tears that fell. She did love loving him. And in the core of her heart, having a part of them alive and living life with them was one of her greatest desires. But Jack didn't understand everything. Perfect people from perfect families rarely did. This was for their own good.

———

"Oh, this is my exit." Lilly's voice jolted Rose back to the snug environment she knew. She slowed and drove them off the highway, softly rubbing her cashmere wrap with one hand. "Turn right on this first street here," Lilly said, pointing.

Rose turned onto a small strip of road with ten double-wide trailers neatly lined in a row. She pulled in front of Lilly's. The trailer had a white picket fence around a small yard, and a white iron table on a porch that extended from the front. It was quaint and neat. Just like Lilly.

"Well, I'm not sure why our paths crossed today, Rose,

but I hope we meet again someday. You've been mighty kind to me and little Jack here," she said, reaching for the car door.

Rose got out and walked around to help. Surely Lilly trusted her enough to carry something to the door of the house now. Lilly lifted Jack from the backseat and left the diaper bag for Rose. As they walked to the door, Lilly scrounged for her keys while balancing Jack in her arms. Upon their retrieval, she opened the front door and carried Jack inside. She set his car seat on the floor next to a plaid chenille sofa with wooden wraparound arms.

As she took the diaper bag from Rose's hand, she said, "You know, Rose, I'm not sure what your thoughts are on love and children, but if I could just tell you this one thing. These two men are the best things that have ever happened to me. I used to be afraid, you know." She looked down and ran her fingers across the frayed edge of the diaper bag handle.

"Afraid of what?" Rose asked.

"Afraid of what kind of mother I'd be. Afraid Walter would leave. Afraid Jack would die or something, and I'd be convicted of his murder and sent to rot away in prison with weird women and bad food."

Rose laughed. Lilly certainly had a way of expressing herself.

"I know," she laughed. "I'm kooky that way. But one day, Walter looked at me and said, 'Lil'—that's what he calls me, Lil. He said, 'Lil, you can live your life afraid and end up with nothing. Or you can just take a leap off that cliff of fear you're hanging on and let me catch you. I promise what's waiting at the bottom is worth the fall.' Ain't that poetic?"

Rose felt a burning in her nose. There was no way she was about to cry. Rose didn't cry. Well, not anymore. "I'd say that's rather poetic."

Then Rose just stood there. Stood there staring at Lilly. Staring at her hair, thinking how much darker it looked inside than it had outside in the bright light. Thinking how much bluer her eyes seemed. Thinking how odd that someone with such dark hair would be named Lilly. Thinking of anything other than what Lilly had just said.

"What? Do I have food in my teeth or something?"

Rose blinked. "No, none that I can see." She turned around and opened the door. "Nice to meet you, Lilly."

"I can't thank you enough, Rose."

"You've thanked me, Lilly. You've thanked me."

Rose didn't look back. But she had a feeling she would remember Lilly and Jack for a long time.

On the porch she noticed a box marked "Christmas Decorations" sitting in the corner. Rage began in the very depths of her heart and, as if funneled through each vein, coursed through her, returning her to the woman she was at eight o'clock that morning. Before Lilly. Before an iced Coke and boiled peanuts. Before checkers and Red Light, Green Light. Before Billy Monroe and making love to her husband. Back to the Rose she knew she was now.

She grabbed the edge of Lilly's railing to steady herself.

The smells of burned dinner and her mother's fragrance. The feelings of anger and loss and fear. The sound of the door as it shut quietly yet completely. The cradling of Christopher's arms around her as she wept beside the box of Christmas decorations that held unpacked garland and wreaths and memories. And each sound and smell and emotion came rushing back at her as if the wind were trying to swallow her whole.

"Are you all right, Rose?" Lilly's voice stopped the barrage.

Rose worried that her knees would give way before she made it to the bottom step, but she steadied herself, forcing pride and confidence to clear her mind, straighten her posture, and return her sanity. "Yes, I'm fine," she said without turning around.

———~———

Lilly watched as the luxury automobile carried the desperate soul to who knew where. Lilly looked at her little angel sleeping soundly beside the recliner. She sat down and called Walter again. He hadn't even returned from lunch yet, so she told them not to bother him with her previous message. They could take care of their car when he got home.

She looked at the diaper bag. She knew what was in it and what that offered. But something about today tugged at her to finally let go. She knelt down, quietly unzipped the diaper bag, and pulled out the bottle that had been snugly stowed beneath the tiny diapers. She stood and studied the bottle's amber liquid. And made a decision. It was time to do what Walter encouraged—let go of that cliff. With determination she walked over to the sink, unscrewed the cap, and watched as the liquor disappeared. She threw the bottle into the trash.

The *Streams in the Desert* devotional Walter had given her the previous Christmas was sitting on the small glass table beside the recliner. She went to sit down and carefully turned to that day's devotion. It was all about the fragrance and beauty of a rose. She wrote inside the pages about the stranger she had met. And when she was through, she closed the book and leaned her head back on the worn velvet fabric. She closed her eyes, thankful for her still-sleeping child. And in the quietness of her soul, she whispered the name Rose over and over again to the only One who could truly catch her when she fell from that increasingly slippery cliff. And then Lilly prayed that someone was waiting for her at the bottom of her cliff as well.

6

"Where have you been?" Helen scolded.

"I picked up a stranger," Rose said flatly.

"You did what? Are you crazy? Do you have fever? Did you break down and eat beef on one of your overseas trips? Because this sounds exactly like what my friend Jeanine's friend Lenora said her cousin twice removed was like when she got mad cow disease."

Rose shook her head, keeping her eyes on the road. "I'm pretty certain I don't have mad cow disease."

"Well, what about the e-mail? And if you tell me you still haven't read it, I will know that you do officially have some type of degenerative brain disease, or either this trip is about far more than you've been telling."

"No, Helen, I have not read your e-mail—"

"You—"

"But," Rose interjected quickly, interrupting Helen, "I had to help a lady who was stranded. So I haven't had time. But I will next time I stop." She refused to tell Helen she'd already stopped.

"Well, say what you will, but I'm calling the doctor and making you an appointment as soon as you get home."

"I don't need a doctor," she said. To herself she added, "Doctors can't fix my broken."

———⌣———

The tiny red message light on the top of Rose's BlackBerry was blinking. As she drove back onto the interstate, she began to scroll through the caller ID to see who she had missed. There were four calls from Helen—all in the span of the ten minutes she had been inside Lilly's—plus the fifth one she had just endured. One call from Max. And one from the senator.

Not the senator who had just suggested she pay him for his support of her bill. No, this was *her* senator. She felt the tires slide off the road and looked up in time to jerk the car back onto the highway.

"You've got to pay attention," she scolded herself. It was a miracle she had never been in an accident before. She dialed her voice mail.

The familiar voice came over the speakers in the car. "Hey, it's me. You've probably already heard about what the opposition is trying to do. But don't worry, you've worked hard, so we'll figure out something while you're gone."

He paused.

"I know you had to go and do what you're doing, though I'm not quite sure what that is, seeing as you haven't told anybody. I couldn't even get anything out of Helen."

That was no big surprise. Even if Helen had known, she wouldn't have told him, what with the way she felt toward him.

"But I miss you already. Plus, she isn't coming back to town at all until after the holidays. And I don't have to leave for another week. So when you get home, take a couple of mental-health days and come spend them with me."

Rose deleted the message. And somewhere inside, down past the parts that X-rays can find, where feelings dwell, she wished she could delete all the things she had tried to hide.

Rose straightened the collar of her new Ralph Lauren suit, blue with fine white pinstripes. The white silk camisole that peeked out from underneath the jacket was just right, but it was the large burnt-orange flower she had pinned on that accentuated the tones of her hair.

The Capitol still filled Rose with amazement. Two centuries of American history and the finest democracy in the world still held the power to amaze even though she knew that none of it, unfortunately, could escape the politics.

She approached Senators Alex Carmichael and Richard Waterstone. They were standing beside the *Conflict of Daniel Boone and the Indians* sculpture in the Capitol Rotunda, one of the three public areas of the second floor of the Capitol, and the same floor as the chambers of the House of Representatives and the Senate. The imposing grandeur of the Capitol threatened to overwhelm them. But the surroundings couldn't quite squelch the senators' conversation.

Alex's hands flailed with drama, animating every word. Richard stood calmly beside him, hands in the pockets of his fifteen-hundred-dollar charcoal gray suit with rich olive green tie. Rose had met them both last session.

"Rose, you look lovely today," Alex said, interrupting himself, then leaned over to kiss her on the cheek.

"Nice to see you, Senator Carmichael."

"Rose, thanks for being willing to meet with me today," Richard added as he patted her arm. His requests to meet with Rose had been more and more frequent. They both said it was because of the new legislation they were trying to push through before they recessed for the summer. They both would not say that the time spent together had changed the atmosphere between them. Yet as the distance between herself and Richard had closed, the distance between herself and Jack had only grown.

"Let's walk," he said, motioning in front of them.

"It looks like we're going to get some unmerited opposition," Alex said as they walked. "Not what we need."

Rose looked at him. "Is it negotiable, maneuverable?"

"I'm not sure. It's coming straight from the White House."

Rose smiled. She saw Richard eye her but ignored it. "Senator Carmichael," she said, the sound of her heels reverberating through the Rotunda, "when have we let something like a president thwart our purpose? In fact, just the other day I heard he was actually talking about what we were doing." She winked.

"No, he was talking about what *you* are doing and what *you* have been getting accomplished up here," Alex replied.

"Well, then we'll just get us an audience with the president if need be."

Richard laughed and tilted his head toward Alex. "She makes you think you can do just about anything, doesn't she?"

Alex patted her on the back like a school buddy. "Yes, I do believe, Miss Rose, for such an unassuming lady, you aren't intimidated by much."

"They don't pay me to be intimidated," she confirmed.

Alex laughed. Their short journey had brought them to another entrance to the Rotunda. "Well, you two mull over some creative strategies, and I'll go work the floor," Alex said. "I'm good at that."

Rose and Richard watched Alex leave, his departure causing an awkward moment.

To Rose's relief, Richard asked, "Got time for lunch?"
"I'm starved."

~

Richard pulled his black Mercedes convertible underneath the
stone portico of the Hay-Adams. Rose loved the hotel, a
Washington landmark built in the 1920s, not only for its history and beauty but also for its wonderful food. As for the
prestige part, well, she enjoyed that too.

Rose frequented the hotel weekly, for lunch or dinner or
both. In fact, she first met Richard there after a lunch she'd
had with another senator. She had always gone dutch. It
was an ethics thing. Before ethics between lobbyists and
government officials mattered to few in Washington besides
herself.

The valet helped Rose slide out of the car. The rich mahogany wood-and-glass door welcomed them. Rose admired
Richard as they entered. He was a towering figure at six foot
two. But Jack's six-foot frame had also made Rose feel the
power of his presence. Both men had professional power in
their own right as well. Richard in the halls of Congress. Jack
in his position at the State Department.

They walked from the rich mahogany tones of the lobby
into the cool creams of the Lafayette Room, where all the dining experiences at the Hay-Adams took place. The maître d'
led them—amid smiles and warm greetings—to a quaint

table for two, with a window view that revealed the most majestic destination in North America: the White House. The awe it invoked in Rose couldn't be tarnished by whoever lived there. If you made it to the White House, an automatic level of respect came with your arrival.

Richard fumbled with his black leather briefcase as they took their seats. Rose noticed his nervousness. "Are you okay?"

He pulled a folder out and placed it at the edge of the table. He ran his index finger down the edge. "Yeah, it's just been a little frustrating around here lately."

She laid her cream linen napkin in her lap and smoothed it across her legs, appreciating that, unlike cheaper fabric, the linen wouldn't leave white fuzz on her navy suit when she left. "I know exactly what you mean."

He took a drink of his water, then gazed directly into her eyes. "Well, unfortunately, frustration around here leads to frustration at home."

She studied him, remembering the explosion that had occurred that morning after Jack discovered her deception. The confrontation had left her reeling and angry and, well, frustrated herself.

The waiter and the food distracted them. Over Rose's lavish vegetarian lunch, she watched Richard eat his "Uncobb" seafood salad. She recalled the fact that Jack had never once ordered just a salad. As an accompaniment to a steak maybe, but never just a salad.

Conversation about the legislation, the obstacles, the resources—these familiar topics allowed their comfortable rapport to return. Before long, lunch was over, and the staff was ready to prepare for dinner.

"Want to finish up back at the office?" Richard asked.

"Sure. I think we have a few things left to define more clearly."

Upon their arrival at the Russell Senate office building, they found Richard's staff working diligently. They retreated to his office, where he promptly made himself comfortable on the small, deep gold velvet sofa sitting in the center of the room. He clasped his hands behind his head and stretched.

Rose sank down at the other end of the couch, which wasn't far, and sighed as the cushions gathered around her body. She crossed her legs, which caused the strap of one Prada shoe to slip from her ankle. The shoe dangled lightly, but she made no attempts to adjust it.

"I think my wife is having an affair," Richard announced suddenly, sitting forward and piercing her with his deep green eyes. He had mentioned his family before, but neither of them had talked much about their spouses or deeply personal things. He rested his forehead in the palm of his hand. "I'm never home," he said as he ran his hand through his thick, wavy brown hair. Traces of gray in his hair and manicured goatee hinted at the labor and toil of a senator. "Who can blame her for finding someone who actually has time for her?"

"Are you really sure?" Rose asked, leaning in, revealing her concern. "I mean, maybe it's not what you think."

"I'm pretty certain. She hasn't taken great pains to keep it a secret," he said, kicking his shoes off and planting his gray-socked feet on the polished coffee table in front of them. It was already getting dark outside, so he turned on the lamp that sat on the end table.

"Well, if she's not trying to hide it, then she must be desperately trying to get your attention."

"Is that what affairs are about? Getting attention?"

"I'm not sure. I'm sure affairs happen for multiple reasons, but it might be in this case. Especially if you never have time to be with her."

"Well, if that's true, she hasn't exactly chosen the best method," he said. "But we've never had much of a marriage. Three kids have kept us together, but the last one leaves the nest next year, and I doubt we'll have much to hold on to after that. We will have done our job."

Rose could see hurt beyond his exterior, his masculine pride. At least she thought it was hurt. She instinctively laid her hand on his arm. As soon as she did it, she knew it was a mistake. But it was just an action of consolation. She removed her hand and let her words do the soothing instead. "I'm sorry for what you're going through."

They sat in silence until an interruption by a secretary roused them back to work. They spread out their notes on a table situated below a painting and sconces that offered the perfect amount of light. And to Rose the next few hours played out in exponential speed, because the secretary's next visit asking if it was okay if she could go home announced the late hour.

"Ten o'clock! I can't believe that much time has passed," Rose said, yawning. "Another long day."

"Yeah, that's all I seem to have is long days. Shoot, I'd probably have an affair on me too." Richard laughed.

Rose bent over and slipped her shoes back on. She had rid herself of them somewhere between hours two and three. She closed her leather notepad and placed it inside her briefcase, which she had placed beside her chair. "You shouldn't say that. No one should have to go through that. And she shouldn't allow you to suffer that way. It's not right."

Richard leaned across the table and was staring at her when she raised her head back up. His nearness startled her. "You want to go have a drink with me? Get some dinner?"

She recognized immediately what he was asking. Both his eyes and the way he said it made the message perfectly clear. And she knew that everything she hated was wrapped up in his request. Yet Richard understood her. She understood him. And he was hurting. They were both hurting. And, well, Jack was so angry with her, he'd probably be asking for a divorce by next week anyway.

As her mind raced, deep in the recesses of her soul she felt a tug. A familiar yet distant tug. It pricked at her conscience and gave a pull on her heart. Rose wanted to follow it. She had always wanted to follow it. But it demanded so much. So much she couldn't control.

"I like expensive wine," she toyed.

"I know."

As they walked out the door, she could sense the abyss before her—one they would never return from. It would change them both forever. Yeah, she knew all of that. Richard closed the door behind them, and she noticed his manicured hand. Rose dove anyway.

———

"I got your message," Rose said to Richard's voice mail. She stared at a green Tahoe with North Carolina plates, which made her realize that she must be about through Virginia. "I can't wait to see you either. And I think it's time that we make some really clear choices."

He would know what she meant. And she had already decided there was no going back. Because going back would be far more difficult than continuing forward. Even if forward took her right off the edge of a cliff. What did Lilly know anyway?

7

"Where are you now?" Charlotte asked in no fewer than ten syllables.

"You're as bad as 'Are we there yet?' But I've had a couple of interruptions on the way. I think I'm somewhere near the North Carolina border, though I don't think anyone's going anywhere."

"Well, you're right about that. And we're still missing a few people. But Uncle Talmadge and Aunt Norma just came in with Priscilla and Presley."

That meant the decibels at Mamaw's house had just gone up by ten. Everyone in that family talked as though everyone else was deaf. "Have those children ever actually forgiven their parents for naming them such names?"

She could tell Charlotte was taking a moment to check out

the situation and see. "Well, by their expressions, I don't think so. Oh, and Uncle Furliss just got in, and by the way his face looks, I'm certain he's gone under the knife again."

"What's that make, five, six?"

"Seven, but who's counting?"

"So who else is missing?" Rose asked.

"Oh, I think we're missing Uncle Preston and Aunt Jewel." Charlotte paused. "Yeah, they're still not here because there aren't any deviled eggs yet. That's all we let Aunt Jewel bring—her deviled eggs. We tell her it's because they're so good, but it's because it's the only thing that she makes you can actually keep down."

Rose laughed. And Aunt Darlin isn't here yet either, and then who knows what cousins are coming. *What?*" Charlotte yelled into Rose's ear.

"I didn't say anything."

"I'm not talking to you. Aunt Norma's screaming at me. This place is like a truckload of banty roosters let loose. Oh no, honey child, she's walking this way with her arm stuck out. I think you're about to get another greeting."

"Charlotte . . . no . . . please, I don't—"

"HI, DEAR."

"Hello to you too, Aunt Norma."

"WHERE ARE YOU, SWEETIE?" Rose turned down the volume on the car phone. "I KNOW YOUR MAMA CAN'T WAIT TO SEE YOU. SHE SAID SHE HASN'T SEEN YOU IN YEARS. NOW, SWEETIE, IT JUST AIN'T RIGHT NOT TO SEE YOUR MOTHER. BUT

YOU BE SAFE, NOW, WITH YOUR DRIVING AND ALL. WE'LL BE HERE WAITING FOR YOU. IS JACK WITH YOU?"

Rose's pulse hammered. She hoped that if she didn't say anything, maybe Aunt Norma would just ask another question.

"ROSEY, DID YOU HEAR ME? IS JACK WITH YOU?"

"Aunt . . . ma . . . break . . . up . . . hear . . . me?"

"ROSEY!" Aunt Norma screamed. Rosey turned down the volume farther. "ROSEY, CAN YOU HEAR ME? ROSEY?"

"He . . . Nor . . ." she tapped the phone with her manicured nail.

She heard the clatter as Aunt Norma handed the phone back to Charlotte. "I DON'T KNOW WHY YOU YOUNG'UNS WASTE YOUR TIME ON THOSE CONFOUNDED CELL PHONES. YOU CAN'T EVEN TALK TO PEOPLE ON THEM ANYWAY."

"Rosey, are you there?" Charlotte asked.

"Yeah, I'm here."

She snorted. "You are pathetic. Anyway, you need to hurry your little self up. Besides, sanity is getting harder and harder to find."

"Isn't Christopher there yet?" Rose asked. When it came to sanity, he was the only one she knew who actually had it.

"No, I haven't seen hide nor hair of him or his bride yet. I hear she's pregnant."

Rose's heart grew heavy. "Yeah, she's going to have a little girl." She changed the subject. "Well, I'm on my way. I'll be there eventually."

Charlotte's tone changed. "You okay, Rose? Your voice, well, you just sound really tired."

Rose glanced at her reflection in the rearview mirror. Dark circles under her eyes had become more common over the last couple of years. The sleep she used to think she didn't need and didn't avail herself of now simply didn't come at all. Her mind was too keyed up and fractured. And if she did fall asleep, she only prayed she didn't wake up in the middle of the night. Because nothing had the power to get her back to sleep if she did. "I'm fine," she finally said, pinching her cheeks, trying to produce some color.

"Well, I don't believe you, but you always were a pitiful liar."

"I take offense to that."

Charlotte laughed. "Take offense all you want, but you gave us away more times than I can count." Rose could imagine her dressed in pink. Charlotte always wore pink. And she was probably leaning against the curve of the kitchen counter, twirling the long phone cord that stretched across the entire room. Charlotte refused to buy a cordless. Aunt Norma had convinced her they caused brain tumors.

"I did it for our own good," Rose assured her. "Or we would have ended up wretched."

Charlotte sucked her teeth. She probably had a toothpick in her mouth. "Most people think we hairdressers are wretched, the way we gossip."

"Well, most people think we lobbyists are wretched too. So

I guess I didn't save us from people's perceptions, but maybe I saved us from ourselves."

"Uh-oh, we better hang up. Uncle Talmadge is headed this way now, with your mother tight on his heels."

"Bye," Rose said.

"I'll call you later."

———

"Mamaw and Granddaddy are watchin' *The Price Is Right*," Charlotte informed Rosey from her perch on the top step of their grandparents' porch. "They won't know we've gone anywhere for a good hour." She twirled her blonde ringlets while chomping on a piece of Hubba Bubba. Strawberry, to be exact. Because it was pink.

"But where do we get them?" Rosey asked as she straightened the belt to her size 10 jeans. Her little legs were growing, though not quite fast enough. So her mother still had to hem all of her pants. At least her sizes were keeping up with her age. She would be out of juniors in four years. She hoped.

"Christopher and Bobby Dean said that the gas station— the one you can see through the field—will sell them to us."

Rosey stared at the mischief maker beside her. "We're ten years old! They're not going to sell us cigarettes."

Charlotte stuck out her chest and straightened her own jeans. "We don't look ten. We look at least twelve."

"So they'll sell them to twelve-year-olds?"

"Well, Bobby Dean's only twelve and a half, and Christopher's only thirteen and a half, so I'd think we stand a good chance."

Rosey picked up her purse. It was made with blue linen needlepoint and round wooden handles. It had been a gift for her birthday. "I've only got a dollar," she said after rooting around for change. With bare feet she tapped the wood step below the one that she sat on. She never wore shoes unless forced.

Charlotte picked up her matching purse, because she always had to get whatever Rosey had gotten. Except her purse was pink. "I've got fifty cents. But I don't even think they cost a dollar, so we've got plenty. Now, come on," she said, standing up and grabbing Rosey's hand.

Scout rose up from his resting position, where he had been twitching his ears against the periodic flies. "Scout can come with us!" Rosey said. She felt sin was accomplished better with multiple partners.

"You think he'll tell anybody?" Charlotte questioned.

"He's a dog, Charlotte. He ain't gonna tell a soul," Rosey assured her, though in her heart, it felt wrong. Away they tromped anyway, down the street and through the partially mowed field. Rosey regretted her idea to have Scout follow them. He was Granddaddy's baby. And if her granddaddy knew what she was doing, he'd be so disappointed. But if he knew that Scout had been party to their excursion, well, she had no idea what he would do. But she did know exactly what her mamaw would do. The tree with all the missing limbs, the one she'd labeled the switch tree, testified to what Mamaw would do.

An acne-covered teenager stood behind the counter, with a wad of chewing tobacco sloppily placed in the left side of his jaw. By the looks of him, Rosey didn't figure he would care if they had slapped a case of beer on the counter.

Charlotte and Rosey fumbled over what kind of cigarettes they wanted. Charlotte thought the gold package looked sophisticated. Rosey just kept fidgeting with her jeans and elbowing Charlotte to hurry up. Finally, the experienced one behind the counter slapped a pack of Virginia Slim Menthol Lights in front of them. Obviously that's what all the ladies ordered, the two girls convinced themselves.

Scout followed the girls back into the field and toward two large oak trees with expansive trunks that sat on the edge of the property. This spot was far enough away from the store and yet also shielded from the street and the homes nearby.

Rosey sat down, wedging her behind into a niche between protruding tree roots and resting her back against the trunk. Scout plopped himself beside her. She watched as Charlotte got all giddy pulling out the cigarettes from the brown paper bag. Then Rosey realized their oversight. "We can't smoke these. We ain't got no matches." Fortunately, Charlotte never thought of everything when it came to their mischief, and Rosey felt a mixture of disappointment and relief.

But a knowing little smirk covered Charlotte's face, and she pulled out a lighter from her purse. Well, maybe there were surprises left in the world. "I stole it from Bobby Dean. Here, put some of this on," she said, handing a tube of pink lipstick to Rosey.

Rosey frowned. "What do I need lipstick for?"

Charlotte shook her head. "It's what the movie stars do. They have really bright lipstick, and it leaves these rings around their cigarettes. If we're gonna do it, we need to do it right."

Rosey just stared at the pink tube. Poisonous Pink. She figured the name suited perfectly because hell was poisonous too, and that's where they were headed after this anyway.

Charlotte suddenly grabbed the lipstick from her hand. "Well, I'll do it if you don't wanna."

Rosey watched as Charlotte painted the pink all over her lips. She didn't have a mirror, but that fact didn't seem to bother her a bit. Rosey became convinced that if the cigarettes didn't kill them, when someone got ahold of Charlotte with her Jezebel lips, they could pretty much call it done.

"My side, you'd think they made these things childproof," Charlotte said, tugging ineffectually at the cellophane encasing the pack of cigarettes.

Rosey snatched them from her hand and yanked the wrapping off herself. As soon as she finished, the knot in her stomach tightened. But she just kept her eyes on Charlotte and her lips steady, trying not to reveal her fear. Rosey looked at Scout. The old hound seemed to be studying Charlotte too. Rosey rubbed the top of his head, as if trying to apologize to him with each stroke.

"Well, it's about time," Charlotte said, jerking the pack back from Rosey.

Rosey had never seen the inside of a cigarette pack. Now, chewing tobacco she knew. Her granddaddy had cropped tobacco since he was a teenager, and most of his boys still had a hankering for the stuff. Her mamaw had even been a snuff dipper back in her day, but when she found salvation, all the tobacco left the house.

But cigarettes had never been a part of Rosey's world. Salvation had hit their house before Rosey was born, so the stuff had always been banned. She watched as Charlotte lifted the small cardboard top to expose the aluminum-foil wrapping. Behind that was a line of what looked like the bottoms of white crayons.

Charlotte fingered one out carefully.

"You act like you've done this since you were a child," Rosey surmised.

Charlotte ignored her. Her lips pursed as she balanced the narrow world of sin between her two scrawny fingers, nails encrusted with dirt from their earlier project of mud pies. Christopher had shown them a new technique—adding milk. Unfortunately, about that time Mamaw caught them with her milk jug. That's why Christopher and Bobby Dean were still at the house. They had been punished with a full hour of *The Price Is Right*.

Charlotte brought the white stick up to her pink-covered lips. She flicked the lighter. It blew out. "C'mon, you silly goose."

Rosey wouldn't have been surprised if Charlotte had cussed, except that Charlotte's mother had overheard her last go at profanity and washed out her mouth with soap. Charlotte must've learned to tame her vocabulary.

Rosey inwardly prayed the lighter wouldn't work at all, but then the flame caught the end of the cigarette. Obviously she hadn't prayed loud enough. Because she was certain by the "all pray" at her church that the louder you prayed, the better God heard. At least she figured that was the reason they all prayed at the same time. Maybe that explained why most of her family talked so loud too.

Her thoughts came out aloud. "You reckon God hears louder prayers?"

Charlotte crinkled her nose at Rosey. "Why are you going and talking about God when I'm trying to smoke here, Rosey?" Charlotte opened her pink lips wide and placed the cigarette between them, pressing tightly around the end. Then she took a big ol' puff off that cigarette. Rosey watched as Charlotte's eyes widened and smoke came rolling out of every orifice except her eye sockets.

She hacked and coughed and hacked and coughed. Scout sat up and was about to pat her on the back himself when she finally straightened up and said, "Wow, that was amazing! Here, you try." She stuck the cigarette out in front of Rosey. The shade of green Charlotte had turned caused Rosey more than a moment of concern.

Rosey tried to scoot back, but the tree resisted. "I'm not letting that stuff come out of my nose like that! You looked like a train! Plus, didn't you know you weren't supposed to inhale?"

"What's inhale?" Charlotte asked, her eyes now watering.

Rosey shook her head and took the pink-smeared stick from Charlotte's hand. "It's what you just did. Breathing it all into your lungs and stuff. You just put it between your lips and suck it into your mouth and blow out lightly."

"How do you know?" Charlotte challenged.

"I've seen Christopher do it, out by the lake. Like this," she said.

Rosey could taste the waxy lipstick. She breathed a little smoke into her mouth and then blew it right back out in Charlotte's direction. Rosey figured she looked like a pro on the outside. But she felt horrible inside.

"That's amazing," Charlotte offered.

"Well, that's how it's done." And Rosey handed the cigarette back to Charlotte to allow her to die in her sin.

Charlotte placed it carefully back between her fingers. "You remember when we had to go to the nursing home to see Aunt Neiva, and that old lady in the wheelchair thought we had stolen her snuff?" Charlotte snorted as she puffed and then blew out lightly.

"You did steal her snuff," Rosey stated matter-of-factly.

"But it was funny watching her yell at us, because she didn't have a tooth in her head."

"Maybe that's why she liked the snuff."

Charlotte nodded at the reasonableness of the evaluation. "Yeah, maybe that is why she liked it. She could just gnaw it."

Rosey's stomach churned at the thought. But she just sat there and watched as Charlotte finished off the cigarette all by herself, never seeming to care that Rosey didn't partake again. She even reapplied her lipstick a couple of times during the process. Finally, Charlotte put out the cigarette at the base of the tree, and then they found a safe place to hide their stash underneath the Jacksons' back deck. Rosey would pray for rain, and before night was over she'd tell Christopher. She always told Christopher.

On the return home, Charlotte's green face kept getting greener. "I think I have cancer," she said as she stopped by a tree and threw up. "I read you can get it from these things," she said with her head still between her legs. Rosey patted her on the back.

Charlotte finally straightened up to finish their journey home. "Yeah, I'm sure I've gone and given myself cancer. My mama's gonna kill me."

Rosey was pretty certain it was all true.

8

Rose had her car cleaned once a week, whether it needed it or not. A mobile car-washing service came to her house and detailed it for the pleasant sum of a hundred dollars. Others paid a hundred and fifty, but she was a loyal customer. A loyal yet particular customer. They couldn't use anything that was greasy or had an odor. She liked the smell of the new leather and didn't want anything taking away from what her money had afforded her.

After all, she had worked hard for it. During the first few years of their marriage, she and Jack struggled while she made a name for herself in Washington. But his promotions within the Department and her steady rise within her own company made the Cape Cod seem too small. Rose wanted a new, more substantial home. She didn't like struggling. Nor reminiscing about it. And she didn't like messy.

So when the blackbirds that passed over the interstate deposited remnants of their lunch on her car, she wanted to cuss. But she was a lady. And ladies didn't cuss. That's what her mamaw told her anyway. Plus, she had met her quota before she even made it to the interstate. She was grateful her mamaw didn't know some of the other things she did now as well.

She hit the washer-fluid button, and the wipers immediately came on. They failed to rid the windshield of every trace of the bombers, but she wasn't completely frustrated about it. After all, it did take her back again to Billy Monroe.

———

"What'd ya eat for dinner?" Jenny asked as she came out of her front door and sat on the steps to strap up her sandals.

Rosey had taken off her church dress with complementing shawl and slipped on some white denim shorts and a little T-strap top with yellow polka dots on the front. "Oh, the usual. Fried chicken, rice and gravy, some butter beans and corn, and homemade biscuits."

Jenny tugged at her strap. "Why doesn't your mama ever cook for you?"

"I don't know," Rosey said, having never really thought about it. "We just always go to Mamaw's for dinner."

Jenny hopped up from the step. "Even during the week?"

"Well, not every night during the week. But most nights. I mean, have you ever tasted anything my mama's cooked? It's really pretty gross," Rosey said, starting toward the river. "So what do you think Billy wants to do at the river anyway?"

Jenny widened her dark eyes at Rosey. "Silly goose, he wants to kiss you."

Rosey's face registered horror, but she recovered quickly. "You think?" she added nonchalantly.

"That's what all boys his age want. At least that's what my mama says. And that's what Stephen at school has been trying to get me to do all year. But I told him, these lips weren't made for kissing; they were made for—" She stopped and looked at Rosey.

Rosey tugged at her arm. "Made for what? What did you tell him?"

Jenny's face blushed. "Made for singing."

"Well, I'll agree with you there. In fact, how 'bout you and me make a deal. If I die before you, promise that you'll sing at my funeral. Because with the way you sing, I bet Jesus would come flying in on an angel or something."

Jenny nudged Rosey's shoulder with her own. "I'd be honored to sing at your funeral."

"Plus, with all the sinning Charlotte does around our house, it ain't a real bad idea to have someone getting us closer to heaven."

"Maybe I should sing at her funeral too."

Rosey could surely agree with that one. "That might even be more important than singing at mine. I'm not sure if Jesus will be showing up any other way."

"So back to the kissing," Jenny said.

"Well, I'm not afraid to kiss him," Rosey said with a shake of her head.

"Oh, well ain't you Miss Brave Pants. 'I'm not afraid to kiss him,'" she mocked, sticking her nose up in the air as they reached the end of the street, where a trail between two houses led to the river.

Rosey put her hands on her hips and stopped. "Well, I'm not."

"Rosey Lawson, you ain't ever kissed a boy in your life! You know you are shakin' in your sandals. Now, come on."

Before she started walking again, Rosey gave Jenny her most mature expression. After all, she *was* maturing—she was actually starting to wear shoes. "Just because I haven't kissed a boy doesn't mean I'm afraid to. It just means no boy worth kissing has ever showed up."

Jenny grabbed her hand and pulled. As they walked, she asked, "And you think this long-haired drummer boy is worth kissing?"

They scrambled over a fallen tree limb.

"I think he's worth thinkin' about kissing."

"Well, you don't have much time for thinkin' because I

spy with my little eye a long-haired boy headed straight for you."

Rosey looked up from the path and saw the blond tresses bouncing on the shoulders of her heartthrob. Now, granted, she and Jenny would never forget Donny Osmond or Michael Jackson, but neither one of those boys had shown up in the city of Mullins, and truth be told, she wasn't quite sure if they ever would. So there was no reason to waste a perfectly good Billy Monroe.

Rosey's heart started beating fast. Jenny stopped, because Billy now blocked the path. Rosey didn't have to, because one glance had her frozen in place.

"Hey, Billy." Jenny said, breaking the tension that surrounded Rosey's immobilized feet.

Billy's mouth spread into a big, cocky grin. "Hey, Jenny," he said. "Hey, Rosey." He pointed his shining, silver metal smile in her direction as he pushed his sunglasses on top of his head.

That melted her. "Hey, Billy," she whispered back, digging the toe of her sandal into the dirt.

"Well, what a great day for being out here in this beautiful place with all this fresh air," Jenny said, spreading her arms and taking in a big whiff of the air. Air that wasn't as fresh as she had originally thought. "Ooh, might be a skunk nearby," she said, crinkling her nose and coughing.

Rosey didn't pay her any attention. Billy didn't seem to either.

"Well," continued Jenny, "I've been wanting to follow that path over there to see where it leads, so if y'all don't mind, I think I'll just catch up with you later." Away she went, singing to herself.

Billy stuck his hands in the top of his pockets and struck a pose. He flicked his head so a lock of hair flipped to the other side of his face. Unfortunately, that sent his sunglasses flying. He recovered them quickly and returned to his pose. "So you like to climb trees?"

Billy Monroe *and* trees. Rosey couldn't ask for more.

She lived in trees. She and Christopher had created more tree houses in her short years of living than their yard had trees. That's when they moved their building efforts to Mamaw's. "I love to climb trees," she responded, her feet still yet to move.

"Well, this is a great one to climb," he said, pointing and heading over to a big nearby oak that had two limbs protruding over the river.

Finally, she got her legs to work and followed him. Billy climbed up ahead of her. She at first thought it was kind of rude that he didn't stand behind her to help her up, but then she figured he was going ahead of her to make sure she got up safely. Though he never looked back to extend a hand. Well, at least he had asked her to climb it with him.

They sat down side by side on one of the limbs, with their legs dangling over the edge. Rosey grabbed the bark intently so she wouldn't fall into the water below. Because after all, she didn't want to embarrass herself in front of a high schooler. Some things were worse than death, and that would be one of them.

"So how long are you staying around here?" Rosey asked as she slowly began to swing her feet beneath her.

He brought one leg up onto the bark and sat his foot down flat with his knee bent. *It was so manly*, Rosey thought, until he momentarily lost his balance and had to grip the limb with both hands to steady himself. Rosey pretended not to notice, and it didn't take long for him to regain both his composure and his cockiness. "Oh, a couple more weeks. I just came down to see my sister before I go home to Florence and go back to school. I'll be a freshman, you know. And I've already got the place ready to welcome me with open arms. I really am one of the more popular kids in my class."

"But aren't you kind of afraid of being in such a big place with older kids?" She swung her legs around and straddled the limb, then put her hands in front of her, since she couldn't think of anything else to do with them.

He made a puffing sound. "They ain't nothin' to be scared of. They're just a bit bigger than me, but I could take on any of 'em."

Rosey was certain he could. With his long, gangly arms, entire villages could be decimated. She studied his face. Besides a few little pimples on his forehead, he was flawless. And he studied her. She could tell by the way his eyes scanned her. She hoped he thought she was pretty. She knew she wasn't close to high school, yet for today she was here, and other girls weren't.

"So how long have you been playing the drums?" She tried to stay cool.

"Oh, since I was nothin' but a kid. I have a rock band back at home, you know. It's called Billy and the Boys. We meet every Wednesday in my garage, and word around the street has it that we're going to be picked to play for the prom this year."

"Wow, you must be so excited about that."

"Yeah, well, we really are one of the best bands in the city." He blew his scraggly hair out of his face. It fell right back.

Rosey tried not to smile too big. "So do you like it around here?"

He swung his leg to the other side of the tree limb and inched closer. She felt her insides start to swim and realized that maybe Jenny had been right. "Yeah, I like it around here," he said with a smile that raised one corner of his mouth and twisted the other.

He scooted even closer. Rosey had only been this close to a boy one other time. It was last year at school with Sean Patterson. He was the cream of the sixth-grade crop, and crazy about Rosey. He cornered her in the hall one day to try to kiss her. Then a teacher who'd spotted them through the glass pane of her door came to Rosey's rescue. At least that was how Rosey viewed it. Sean and the teacher, however, seemed to have different perspectives.

But something in Rosey felt different today. Excited, curious. She brushed a piece of stray bark from her white shorts. A small brown smudge remained. She looked up at him, then shifted her gaze over his shoulder.

He wasn't deterred. He came closer, and his knees touched hers. "I really like the fact that you're here most of all."

She kept looking over his shoulder. She figured he'd think she was partially blind or cross-eyed, but she just couldn't bring herself to look him square in the face. "Well, uh, it's pretty neat that you're here . . ."

And before she could finish her sentence, he made his move. Almost like a wasp diving in for the sting, and in that moment, fear made its way to the surface. She placed one of her hands firmly on his shoulder, hindering his momentum so that his face slipped past her own. His shoulder hit hers, and they tottered slightly.

Rosey let out a nervous laugh as they both regained their balance. She prayed he'd spend his life thinking he had simply missed her face.

His face began to be swallowed whole by a red sensation that started at his neck and then splotched its way to the top of his head. He swiftly brought their adventure to an end.

"Well, I need to get going. My sister's probably wondering where I am," he said. He swung his legs up and returned to the trunk for his descent.

Rosey's face flushed. She wanted to jerk him back and kiss him smack-dab on the lips. How could she have let the opportunity of kissing such a boy slip away? And more than that, she hated the thought of all the questions Jenny would pummel her with on their walk back home. Rosey slowly lifted herself to start the climb down to where her future husband had paused to brush off his sagging jeans.

"It was really nice of you to ask me out here today," Rosey said to the top of his head. "Maybe we can come out here again next Sunday or something."

He looked up at her and smiled hesitantly. "Yeah, maybe we can do that. Well, I'll see ya later."

Rosey hopped down onto the hard ground. But just before Billy turned to go, as if in slow motion, she felt a warm slathering of something fall across the left side of her head, down onto her left shoulder. By the look of horror on Billy's face, she could've guessed what it was. But Jenny's return saved her the effort.

"Oh my word, Rosey, look at your shoulder. You've just been pooped on by a bird."

Rosey was certain her face had turned the color of her hair. She hoped that would make her blend in with her surroundings and disappear. Billy's lips had distorted in disgust.

Before she could open her mouth, he waved his hand and headed off back to wherever he had come from.

Jenny came around to get a better look at Rosey. "Oh, Rosey," she said, shaking her head.

Rosey just stood there with her hands spread out, not wanting to move. Finally, she brought her left hand to the side of her hair and touched the goo. She gagged immediately.

Jenny took her by the arm and marched her straight to the riverbank and all the way into the water until every gooey bit was floating downstream. And once Rosey recovered from the horror of the moment and the likely loss of her future husband, she realized that the entire incident had made Jenny forget to ask about the kiss. That was enough to be grateful for.

9

A kid picking his nose in a van loaded down with an entire flock of young'uns brought Rose back to the road in front of her. The vehicle came alongside her, slowly over-taking her, as two of the errant children pressed their faces against the back windshield and stuck their tongues out at her. Rose struck back in perfect Gene Simmons style. She couldn't help it. At first she reminded herself that kids weren't what they used to be. But then she decided monsters like that deserved retaliation. They one-upped her, though, with the finger of choice. Her phone rang before she could respond in kind.

"Hey there, sis. Just wanted to check in and see how the trip is coming."

She loved the sound of this voice. "Odd, actually."

"Odd? How's that?" he asked, the Southern lilt still rich.

On anyone else the sound grated on her, but on him and her mamaw, and even Charlotte maybe, she could tolerate it, because it brought back some wonderful memories. "Oh, nothing worth talking about. Just a bunch of kids acting like, well, kids. Giving me a taste of what you and I tortured people with for years."

"What? Did somebody moon you?" He laughed.

She had forgotten about that particular escapade. "No, no full moon over North Carolina yet."

"So where are you?"

She looked up to gauge the road signs. "Somewhere near the Blue Ridge Mountains, I think . . . To be honest, I have no idea. I do know, however, I have awhile to go."

"Really? I thought you would be pretty close by now. Mom said you left early."

"I'm sure she did," Rose retorted.

"Rose, this is no time to be catty. You need to put your differences away. She's more than paid for what she's done." His tone was different. It was the fathering tone he had attached to her.

Rose tried to hide her disgust. "You and I have a different measure for penance, obviously."

He laughed. "We've always had a different measure for penance."

That was so true.

"Well, if you care to remember, I wasn't the one who discovered that if you swung lizards hard enough, their tails would come off," she baited.

"No, and I wasn't the one who discovered that if you threw lizards hard enough against the side of the house, they'd die," he countered.

The dark cloud brought on by his previous remark dissipated. "I'll never be convinced they were dead. I think they were only stunned."

They laughed together. "I've missed you. It's been too long, Rosey."

She wouldn't correct him. It wouldn't matter anyway. "I've missed you too. But we'll catch up. Maybe we can get away, just the two of us."

"If I can get away from Blaine. Her hormones are killing me. You'll hardly recognize her. Her stomach's grown so much and her face is so puffy, *I* hardly recognize her." She knew he was smiling.

"I do hope you have not shared that observation with her."

"Crazy I am not. A pregnant woman and insults aren't company you want in cramped quarters."

"I'm sorry it's been so long. You and I should make more time for each other. Our worlds don't need to be this busy." She knew even as she said it that it wasn't "their" worlds that had become too busy.

"I'd like that. Maybe this summer we can come up and spend some time with you in DC."

She sat up taller in her seat. "That would be great. And I can take the baby to see the Smithsonian and the Holocaust Museum."

"I'm sure a newborn would love all those things. We'll plan it when you get here. So how much longer do you think you'll be?"

"I'm not sure." She felt the beginning pangs of hunger. "I think I'm going to stop here in a minute and get me something to eat. So, hopefully, no later than seven or so."

"Well, be careful. I can't wait to see you."

"I can't wait to see you either."

———~———

She passed exit sign after exit sign for the next twenty minutes, but not one offered any "real" restaurants. And when Rose got hungry, Rose got irritable. Maybe that was what Helen was talking about. How Rose acted when she was hungry.

The phone rang. It was Helen. Helen already thought she might be telepathic, so Rose wasn't about to tell her she had been thinking about her. Nor would she tell her she hadn't read her e-mail yet.

Rose hit the phone button and started talking before Helen could get a word in. "I'm hungry. I'm irritable. I'm stopping."

All she heard was Helen laughing hysterically before the line went dead.

The red light was blinking on her BlackBerry. She picked it up only to discover she had seven new e-mails. The first of which was the one she promised to read hours ago. She'd just have to get off at the next exit no matter what.

The only item listed on the next restaurant sign was "Diner." In the South, that word had multiple meanings and one constant: grease. Rose hated grease. She did now, anyway. She liked tofu and organic food. Real stuff. Not artificial. She had enough of that in her life. She pulled up to the stop sign at the end of the exit and studied her options. There still remained just one, "Diner." She didn't have a choice. Plus, by this point she probably had ten e-mails to answer.

"Surely diners have salads," she convinced herself as she pulled into the parking lot.

———

Rose studied the other cars, an observation that caused her to park at the far end of the lot in order to prevent at least one side of her car from getting mutilated. The vehicles were, well, used. Granted, tweety bird's lunch still had left a milky fog where her windshield wipers couldn't reach, but that was the extent of her vehicle's appearance issues.

The wind was milder than back in Virginia, but after exiting the car, she still draped her shawl around her shoulders, then grabbed her purse and BlackBerry. She closed the door and pressed the little black button on the door handle, listening as the doors locked with a click. In the windows of the small diner, she could see the tops of diners' heads. She pulled her wrap even tighter around her.

Rose used the edge of her wrap to pull on the metal door handle. She was greeted by a waitress in a white uniform, a white apron with ruffled pink trim, and white nursing shoes, with a pencil stuck behind her ear. The woman, yellow pin curls firmly pressed to her head and black-framed glasses slipping down her nose, ordered Rose, "Grab a seat anywhere, darlin'." Then she added over her shoulder, "I'm Daisy. I'll be with you in a few."

Rose scanned the other diners. They scanned her too. The bills of baseball caps and camouflage caps and orange-billed hats had all risen in virtual unison as she entered the door. Even the cooks had stopped flipping whatever it was they were flipping to take a gander over the stainless-steel counter that would momentarily serve up her meal. The other waitresses, however, didn't pay her a dab of attention.

Rose could hear the grease. It was sizzling. She could smell the grease. She was pretty certain it was bacon. And she could see the grease. Because everything shone with a light coating.

Rose took a booth for four in the corner. She slid in with ease, a little too much ease. She was certain a layer of grease had just rubbed itself onto her behind. She set her purse and BlackBerry down next to her. She planned to finally check those e-mails—and all the others that had piled up—before Helen initiated a mental evaluation.

Rose's present responsibilities were demanding and costly. And Rose didn't drop balls. She didn't go ten minutes without checking e-mails either, unless she was in an important meeting. And even then, she and Helen had devised a system. She'd place her phone on vibrate and set it in the seat next to her leg. If it went off three times in a row, Rose needed to call Helen. If she couldn't do that, she needed to check her e-mail immediately. Yet somehow today she had lost track of it all for a few moments.

Sixty-something Daisy headed in Rose's direction and tossed her a menu. "Darlin', you just take a gander and I'll be right back witcha."

Rose wasn't sure if she meant she'd be right back "with her" or "right back with a witch." She studied the menu. Just "Diner." Not "Joe's Diner," not "Fred's Diner," not anybody's "Diner." Just "Diner." She unwrapped her paper napkin from around her fork and knife. She wasn't sure where her spoon was, but she figured you probably ate most things with your hands around here anyway. In fact, she wasn't quite sure why they bothered with utensils at all.

She took the edge of her napkin and used it to flip open the menu so she could actually peruse the inside. It featured fried pork chops, fried chicken, fried steak, accompanied by fried okra, fried green tomatoes, fried squash. She scanned the menu for a salad. There was one—covered with cheese, bacon, and eggs.

"Might as well be an omelet," she muttered to herself.

There was another one with fried chicken, cheese, bacon, and eggs.

"My arteries are clogging just reading this."

The final salad offering was covered with ham, cheese, bacon, and eggs.

"Well, at least it isn't fried." This time the older couple in the booth next to her eyed her curiously.

"So what'll it be, darlin'?"

Rose jerked in her seat. She hadn't seen the waitress coming.

Daisy patted Rose's forearm, trying to soothe her next tipper. Her other hand remained hidden underneath a brown plastic tray. "Honey, I'm so sorry. I didn't mean to scare ya. I was just comin' to see if you were wantin' to go ahead and get ya somethin' to eat."

Rose gathered herself. "Oh, well, I was just . . ."

Daisy set down a glass of water in an amber-hued plastic cup and laid a straw beside it. "Would ya like to hear the specials?"

"Oh, you have specials too?" The words came out before she caught herself.

"Darlin', we've got country ham with some red-eye gravy." Rose had never quite figured out what the red-eye in the gravy was. "We've got fried catfish with collards." Of course they did. "And we've got vegetable soup."

"Just vegetables?"

"Whadya mean, just vegetables?" Daisy asked, using the tip of her pencil to scratch her head.

Rose tried not to cringe visibly. "I mean, does the soup have meat in it?"

"Well, yes, darlin', all vegetable soup has meat in it if it's any kind of vegetable soup."

"Well, I think I'll just have a salad with nothing but tomatoes and cucumbers."

Daisy looked up from the notepad she'd started writing on. "You mean you don't want no cheese?"

"No. No cheese, thank you."

"And you don't want no bacon?" Daisy's head tilt reminded her of her granddaddy's hound, Scout, and she tried not to laugh.

"No, no bacon."

"No ham or chicken or nothin'?"

"No, just some lettuce and tomatoes, and some cucumbers, and oh, add some red onion if you have any of those, and I think that's all." She hugged herself, rubbing her hands up and down her arms, still encased in her wrap, as if she were trying to keep herself warm, but she was really trying to keep herself calm.

"So you just want nothing but lettuce and tomatoes and cucumbers, and some onions?" Daisy took her glasses and tipped them to the edge of her nose, causing the bright purple chain they hung from to bounce lightly.

"Well, I'd really like *red* onion if you have it."

Daisy didn't write a thing down; she just looked at her. "Yeah, red onion."

"And do you have any light dressings?"

Daisy put her pencil-holding hand on one hip and repeated the question. "Light dressings?"

"Yeah, not so heavy in fat?" Rose shifted in her seat. Daisy's piercing blue eyes were making her feel as if her requests might be a little foolish for her environment. If the world actually made vegetable soup by its name—with just vegetables—she wouldn't be in this position.

"Darlin'," she said with a genuine smile, "we ain't never had a light dressing around here since the day we opened."

"Well, do you have oil and vinegar?" Rose wasn't sure whether poor Daisy would recover after this.

"Oil and vinegar?" Daisy sighed. "Sure, darlin', if oil and vinegar will make you happy with your rabbit food, Miss Daisy will find you some oil and vinegar." She tucked her notepad into the pocket of her apron and put the pencil back behind her ear. Clearly she wouldn't need notes for this. "I assume you'll want a diet drink too?"

Rose thought for a moment. The memory of that Coke this morning brought something back to her that she had almost forgotten. Home. "Actually," she said, about to surprise herself, "I think I'd like just a Coke. A regular Coke."

Daisy raised one eyebrow high. "I don't think I heard you correctly. A regular Coke? You sure?"

Rose smiled at her. "Yeah, it's been the kind of day that deserves a Coke. I'll have a regular Coke."

"Well, thank the good Lord, I was about to think you had that anorexica thing or something."

Rose wanted to laugh. "No, I'm not anorexic. Just a vegetarian."

"Vegetarian, smegetarian. You just sit here for a few minutes, and Miss Daisy will be right back with you somethin' to eat." Then Daisy winked. But it was the words she added after the wink that made Rose even more nervous. "And who knows, I might even surprise ya."

Rose watched Daisy as she all but skipped back to the counter. The warmth in the place had begun to penetrate Rose's chill, and she loosened the wrap from around her shoulders and let it slide down her back.

The elderly couple scooted their way out of the nearby booth. Rose watched as the gentleman jiggled the change in his pocket and laid out a couple of dollars and some coins for Daisy to gather upon her return. Then he reached into the small pocket on the front of his worn tweed vest and tugged on a chain that held a pocket watch at the end. He opened the watch slowly with shaky hands, studied it, and then closed it gently. He rolled it absently between his fingers.

Rose stared at it. She could hear it ticking from her table, she was certain. At least she thought it was his clock she heard.

10

Rosey saw the glint of the small gold watch from afar. She watched as her granddaddy shut it and placed it back inside his shirt pocket. He and her daddy were standing on the front porch of his and Mamaw's house as she and Charlotte returned from their encounter with the very pit of wickedness.

Fortunately for them, after her bout of upchucking, Charlotte had remembered her Barbie perfume bottle from her magic bag and squirted them like crazy to cover up the smoke. The attempt, however, at removing the Poisonous Pink lipstick from Charlotte's mouth was not quite as effective.

"Where you going?" Granddaddy asked Rosey's daddy.

Taylor walked down the steps and paused at the bottom. "I'm just going to the church for a little while to work on the hymn selection for Sunday." Rosey loved to see her daddy any-time. Except after moments of heathenism. "Hey, baby girl."

"Hey, Daddy," she called and waved.

He waited for them, setting his right foot on the bottom step and placing his hand on his leg. "What have you and Charlotte been up to today?"

They glanced at each other. "Oh, nothing much going on 'round here today," Charlotte assured him. Nothing much but her mischief.

"Well, you two girls have a great afternoon, and don't you drive Granddaddy crazy," he said. Rosey looked beyond her daddy to see her granddaddy grab the arms of his metal rock-ing chair and sit himself down. It was his favorite seat, where he could spend the rest of the day watching the neighbors go by, like he did most days.

"I'm going home for a little while, Rosey," Charlotte said, turning green again.

"I think that might not be such a bad idea," Rosey assured her. "We can play later. Bring your tape recorder over and we can record ourselves singing with Olivia Newton-John and John Travolta." They loved *Grease*.

Charlotte slowly began to jog with only a wave of her hand. Her house was only two blocks over. Rosey figured they would be two of the longest blocks of Charlotte's life.

"Come sit here with Granddaddy, Red." He motioned with a pat on his left knee.

Rosey loved Granddaddy's knee. She had since she was a baby. His thin dark-gray pants and thin button-down white shirts with their small pinstripes always felt soft against her skin. And his suspenders gave her entertainment.

She ran her hand along the porch railing as she meandered toward Granddaddy's knee. Scout lumbered along beside her, sniffing at her shorts. She was growing up now. Ten was ancient to some. But she didn't ever want to get so big that she couldn't sit on his knee anymore. Granddaddy offered a wrinkled hand and she took it, and they both tugged together to pull her weight up on his knee. Once she was planted securely, she took both of her legs and swung them across his other knee.

Scout walked to the other side of the porch and took some long slurps from his freshened water bowl and then came back and laid his long, gangly self beside them.

She grabbed the gold clasp that adjusted the strap on her granddaddy's suspenders and began to move the straps up and down. "So how was *The Price Is Right*, Granddaddy?"

"Oh, you know that Bob Barker. He knows how to put on a good show." His calloused hand patted the top of her knee as he looked straight out in front of him. "Somebody actually won the Showcase Showdown today, and you know your mamaw, she gets so excited when that happens."

Rosey ran her fingers up and down his suspender that she had extended out to its farthest length. "Did they win a car?"

"Two."

She stopped her tugging. "Two? Somebody got two cars at one time?"

"I know. Can you imagine it?" He leaned down and kissed her head.

She straightened his suspender and closed the clasp shut. Then she laid her head on his shoulder and reached around his face to rub the soft part of his earlobe. She had done this since she was a baby too.

"You and Charlotte have you a big time this morning?" She felt the movement of his lips still placed against the top of her head.

Rosey looked down the porch and could see the side of the church. "We had a good time. Charlotte and I always have a good time," she said, still rubbing his ear softly.

"Have you been smoking out there a little today, Red?"

Rosey's fingers froze at the tip of his ear. Panic swept through her, right down to the tips of her bare feet.

"I can smell it all over you. That and Charlotte's Barbie doll perfume."

Rosey felt the sting of tears as they filled her eyes. She sat up and looked straight into the piercing blue eyes of her granddaddy. It wasn't as if she could go anywhere anyway. "Granddaddy, I know . . . I know it's a sin and we're bound for the eternal pits of hell. And it wasn't even that good, but whatever you do, if you have to beat me till the sun comes up, please don't tell Mamaw, and whatever you do, don't tell Mama and Daddy." Her eyes pleaded with her words.

His face was expressionless for a moment. Then, with that soft smile that had been her companion for the last ten years, he patted her head and pressed it back down on his shoulder. "I'm not going to tell anyone what you've done, baby girl. But you need to know that cigarettes can hurt you. And I don't want anything happening to you," he said, going back to rhythmically patting her knee as he rocked.

"But what are we going to do about the hell part, Grand-daddy? I mean, I know today I made the decision to no longer be able to go up to heaven and be with you and Mamaw and Mama and Daddy." She felt a hot tear run down her face. "Now me and Charlotte are going to be the only two in our family having to live with the devil for the rest of our natural-born lives."

She felt his belly shake as he chuckled. He wiped her tears away. "Who made you think smoking a cigarette would make you go to hell, baby girl?"

"That's what the preacher says. He says smokers and liars and adulteresses . . ." She felt his belly shake again. "He said those people are going to hell, and I know I might have told a lie once by mistake, and now I've smoked, and I've got to find out what the adulteresses thing is so I can make sure I at least don't do that." She sniffled.

"Red, you're crazy." He didn't try to hide his laughter now. "You aren't going to hell for smoking."

She sat up and looked at him. "I'm not?" she said, wiping her nose with the back of her hand; then she wiped it on her shorts.

"But you could get to heaven pretty quick if your mamaw catches you wiping your snot on your shorts."

He and Rosey both got a kick out of that. She laid her head back down on his shoulder. "So you don't think this smoking stuff is going to send me to hell, Granddaddy?"

"God looks at your heart, Red. Thank the good Lord, He looks at our hearts."

She wasn't quite sure if that was such a good thing either, because Charlotte had her convinced that her heart was cancer stricken already. "What do you think He sees?"

"I think He sees that you're sorry. That you really don't want to sneak around and do things that are wrong or hide things from us. You're going to have a thousand opportunities in this life, Red, to make good choices or bad choices. And God wants you to make good choices all the time. But when you make choices that aren't the ones you know you should have made, well, if you come back, with your tears, and with your repentance . . ."

"With my what?"

She could tell he was smiling even though she was back to looking at the side of the church. "If you come back saying you're sorry, then He will forgive you. But you have to mean it. It's not about getting Him to forget this time so you can just do it again. That's why I said He looks at your heart. He looks to see what you really mean inside."

"So let me get this straight one more time. You're absolutely certain I'm not going to hell?"

His belly shook once more. "No, Red, I can assure you, you're not going to hell for smoking today with Charlotte."

He felt her exhale against his chest. Then she asked, "How did you know, Granddaddy?"

"Know what, baby girl?"

"Know that I had been smoking."

"I've worked around tobacco all my life, baby girl. It's part of my nose. And there isn't enough of Charlotte's perfume in this world to get rid of that smell."

Rosey let her body relax against her granddaddy's chest. She moved her arm around to get his earlobe again. As she began to drift off to sleep, the thought flitted through her mind that she wasn't sure how everyone would handle the news of Charlotte's cancer, but then the soft ticking of Granddaddy's pocket watch and his gentle rocking drew her to sleep. Charlotte would just have to take care of the rest.

—————

"Here you go, sunshine!" Daisy said, yanking Rose back to the present and the aroma of grease. She set the heaping plate of fried chicken, mashed potatoes and gravy, green beans, and macaroni and cheese down in front of her.

Rose's eyes glassed over at the feast in front of her. "I think you have my order mixed up with someone else's. I'm the salad with the oil-and-vinegar dressing, remember?"

Daisy set down the ice-cold Coke in another amber-tinted glass and laid the straw beside it. "Darlin', I ain't got your order wrong. I need you to trust me. I saw your bones when you came in here. I mean, look at ya," Daisy said, grabbing Rose's wrist. Rose felt the urge to jerk it back, but Daisy's grip was pretty strong. Daisy made a ring around Rose's wrist so that her middle finger could touch her thumb.

"That, my dear, is the wrist of a woman who is in need of fat."

"But I don't eat meat."

"Well, I can tell that by the size of your wrist. And that's part of the problem. Now, you just trust Miss Daisy on this one and eat you some meat, darlin'. It really will be good for you. Everyone needs protein in their system."

"I eat beans for protein," Rose replied curtly.

Daisy lowered her glasses back down on her nose. "Now, listen here, young lady," she said, her voice sounding very much like that of a mother. "You need food. Real food. Not tofu. Not froufrou. Food. And you didn't come in here by accident today. Trust me, by the way you're dressed, I'm certain this ain't a place you would have picked out if you had choices. But you're here because you need to eat. And I'm here to make sure you do."

Daisy set her plastic tray down on the corner of the table, placed her hands on her hips, and tapped her foot. A visual Rose was certain she had seen at some point in her life on a sitcom.

Rose was so shocked that she sat there in complete amazement at the audacity of the stranger staring at her, waiting for her to start eating. People just didn't do this. They didn't challenge her. They didn't tell her what to do. But now, here was this woman still tapping her foot, a woman who probably made less money in a year than Rose made in a month. Rose wasn't sure what made her pick up her fork with its slightly bent third prong and run it through the gravy of her potatoes. She wasn't sure why she did that. But she had a sneaking suspicion she was eating chicken today. Fried chicken.

11

"Baby girl, Mamaw's got your dinner ready," Mamaw called from the front porch. "You and Christopher come in and get washed up. And don't you bring a lizard in here with you either." They waited until the screen door closed behind her to resume their conversation.

"You think he's dead?" Rosey asked, staring at the stiff lizard lying in the grass.

"Well, I think the way you threw him up against the house pretty much did him in," Christopher said, kneeling down to get a closer look.

Rosey squatted and touched the lizard with her finger. It was hard as a rock. "Well, I didn't mean to kill him. You think his mama will come looking for him and be heartbroken when she finds out I killed her baby?" Rosey fought back the tears welling in her eyes.

Christopher just shook his head as he picked up the stiff critter. "I don't know that lizards have mamas."

Rosey blew a stray curl from her face. She stood up, dug her nails into her palms to avoid crying, put those fists onto her hips, and said, "You don't think lizards have mamas? Everything has to have a mama!"

"No, they don't." He looked up at her with a frown. "What does a little six-year-old know? Plus, it seems like I read somewhere they just are dug up out of the ground or something. They call it archaeologisism, or something like that." He stood up next to her and walked over to their box full of still-vibrant yet a few tailless lizards.

Rosey would've challenged him on how a few years gave him so much more wisdom, but she felt too heartsick over the lizard. "So do you think if we put him back in the dirt that maybe he'd come back alive?"

He puckered his lip and shrugged his shoulders. "I think it's worth a try."

Their daddy came up behind them and scooped Rosey into his arms. "What're my babies doing?" he asked, peppering her face with kisses.

"Daddy, stop. I've got to see where Christopher buries the lizard!" she protested, pushing against his chest.

"Okay, okay, let me go watch too."

Their mama came up behind them. "Ooh, what are you kids doing? I hope you haven't been swinging lizards around until their tails come off. That would just be cruel."

With her foot, Rosey tried to push the box housing their evidence a little farther from her mama's view. She and Christopher had tried to keep their lizard excursions secret, but this little burial with Daddy and Mama present wasn't exactly going to help their cause.

Christopher told Rosey, "I'll check back in a couple days, and if he's gone, we'll know his mama won't come looking for us."

She patted Christopher's back to let him know he'd done an excellent job.

Their mama wrapped her arm around Rosey's shoulder. "Come on, sweetheart, let's get washed up for dinner. You heard your mamaw call." She whispered excitedly into Rosey's ear, "I think she made fried chicken."

"Fried chicken!" Rosey said, dancing herself right out of her mother's arms and up the steps. She jerked the screen door open, catching sight of the hole in it and feeling glad that trouble was over. She didn't let the smack of the door against the house stop her as she ran inside. "Mamaw! Mamaw!" she shouted, stopping abruptly, then jumping up and down when she reached the kitchen. "You made my favorite today?"

"Shh, now, baby girl. I made all your favorites today," Mamaw said, laughing. "Now, go get cleaned up so we can enjoy it while it's hot."

Rosey danced to the bathroom, singing at the top of her lungs. An original tune, of course. Rosey was her own composer. She heard Christopher groan, but she ignored him. When she made it to the table, everyone was in their place. And even though Mamaw and Granddaddy had seven other children, it was Rosey's family and sometimes Charlotte's that usually had meals with them. But that was fine by Rosey, especially considering her mama's cooking.

Rosey sat down next to her mama. She took her mama's soft hand in hers and smiled up at her. "I love you, Mama," she said.

"I love you too, sweetheart. Would you like to say grace for us?"

"Sure." Rosey folded her hands and bowed her head. She confidently prayed, "God is great. God is good. Let us thank Him for our food. By His hands we all are fed. Give us, Lord, our daily bread. Amen."

And amens sounded from every corner.

Rosey took a small breast and put it on her plate. It was the one her mamaw always cut just for her, and then she and Christopher got to make a wish and pull the wishbone. Whoever came up with the largest portion would get his or her wish to come true. Rosey and her brother were about even on the winning scale.

Rosey rested her gaze in turn on each person around the table. She noticed for the first time that Mamaw and Granddaddy looked old. Not old in a bad way. Just old in an always-been-old way. Then she looked at Christopher. He was inhaling his chicken and caught her looking. He grinned wide and bugged his eyes out at her. That made her laugh. She and Jenny might be best friends, but Christopher was her *bestest* friend. Then she looked at her mother. How pretty she looked today with her small pearl earrings and pale yellow dress. And her daddy looked so happy at the end of the table. He caught her eye and said, "What are you thinking, baby girl?"

"Nothing," she said with a shrug. And after winning the wishbone contest, she was certain her wish would come true, that they would all always be as happy as they were at this moment around this table. And that the lizard's mama wouldn't come looking for her. And with that, she took a big ol' bite of her fried chicken.

～

Rose felt something touch her hand, and she caught sight of her surroundings. "You better catch that tear, darlin', before it falls onto your empty plate."

Rose felt the cool trail her tear had made on its way to her chin. She saw the napkin that Daisy was holding against her hand and used it to dab her face. Then she looked at the empty plate in front of her. She didn't even remember eating it. But the weight in her gut assured her she had.

"Here you go, sugar. This will help you wash it all down," the other waitress said as she placed another Coke in front of

Rose and removed her empty glass. Her name tag identified her as Delores.

"Where'd you travel to just now?" Daisy asked, slipping into the booth.

Rose hesitated. She didn't like intimate questions. Intimate questions made her uncomfortable. Nor was she crazy about Daisy's intimate proximity. "Oh, nowhere. Just got lost in my thoughts for a moment."

Daisy picked up her glasses hanging from her neck and began cleaning them with the edge of her apron. "Home has a way of doing things to you."

"What makes you think I was thinking about home?"

"Well, the way I see it is like this." She lifted her glasses up to peer through them. Her eyes looked like a fly's. Then she folded them and let them fall to the top of her chest. "That a classy woman like you, with your nice car and pretty clothes, who is trying her best to disguise any hint of a Southern accent, is trying to get away from something, but I have a feeling you're coming instead of going, and that's why your face is looking so troubled. If you were headed out of here, you'd be wanting a piece of everything I've got in here. But you must be headed back in, and that, darlin', is a whole different story."

"I haven't seen my mother in more than ten years," Rose said, gripping the fork still in her hand tightly.

"It's been ten years since you've seen your mama?" That got Daisy's attention, and she leaned onto the table to get a closer look. "How does someone not see their mama for ten years? She must have torn your heart out good."

Rose puffed. She wasn't quite sure she wanted to be psychoanalyzed by Daisy nor why in the world she had shared such an intimate fact. Yet more still flowed. "Well, let's just say she's not the woman I thought she was."

"Well, by george, you better let it go, or you're going to be missing a lot more than fried chicken in your life."

Suddenly the room felt chilled again. Rose put down her fork and brought her wrap back up around her shoulders. "Well, life isn't as easy as you may think it is. Plus, I've dealt with enough issues today. So if you'll excuse me," Rose said, grabbing her things, "I think it's time for me to be headed to my destination."

"It's time for you to head home. You need to call it for what it is."

Rose reached in her bag and took out her matching Louis Vuitton wallet. She pulled out a credit card.

But Daisy had apparently already nodded to Delores, because Delores arrived at that moment to give Rose a big ol' piece of chocolate pie with meringue. Then a clean fork was laid down in front of her, and her dishes, virtually licked clean, were removed from the table. Daisy got up and walked away.

Rose gazed at the chocolate pie in front of her. Daisy was evil. She looked up to spot Daisy as the waitress busied herself at the main counter. Apparently Rose wasn't going anywhere until she ate some chocolate pie.

12

The last time she had gone home, her granddaddy was sitting out on the front porch when she pulled her car into the church parking lot. He had a look on his face as if he were expecting someone. He squinted to try to see who was behind the wheel. Rose watched him in his familiar spot. She hadn't been home to see her grandparents in almost a year. For the first part of their marriage, she and Jack would come and spend time with them almost every six months. Jack adored them, and they adored Jack.

They were such a constant in Rose's life, but this past year had been busy. And if she were being honest, her latest decisions had made her want to hide from those she loved instead of hang around them. Because people who love you can see things that you can hide from everyone else.

But now, with the way things were going with her and Jack, and the weight of the secret that she had been keeping from him, well, it made her want to see the two people who always made life seem okay. She needed them. The girl who would never admit she needed anyone needed these two people desperately. So she had loaded up the car and come home to surprise them.

Her granddaddy's face lit up when he realized who it was. "Mama!" he hollered, raising himself out of his chair as fast as he could. "Red's here, Mama! Red's here!"

Mamaw came barreling out of the house, apron tied firmly around her stomach. Her slippered feet almost caught up with Rose's granddaddy as he did a hobbling jog down the side staircase, tugging on his suspenders at the same time, as if they would hold him upright.

Rose let the emotion saturate her. No one else in this life, except Christopher, of course, seemed to care whether she was around or not. But these two, these two were running. They were running to her. They were excited because she was home. And she fought the tears. She fought them even while she broke into a run of her own.

They all stood there in the parking lot, laughing and blubbering over each other. Then Mamaw interrupted the moment with a swat to Rose's backside.

"Ow! What was that for?" Rose laughed.

"That's for not calling and letting me make something

special for you before you got here." Then she popped her again.

"Ow! And that would be for what?" Rose asked, rubbing her behind.

"That would be for waiting too long to see us! We could have died ten times since you've been here last." Her mamaw straightened her apron and smiled at her.

Rose wrapped her arm around her as they walked toward the house. "You're too ornery to die," she assured her.

Granddaddy wrapped his arm around Rose from the other side, and they all walked up the steps together. "Well, don't let her fool you either, Red. Mama's been cooking all day. Said she had a feeling someone might be coming by." He leaned over and kissed the top of Rose's head. Even at seventy-three, he still towered over Rose's five-foot-seven frame. "And I did too. That's why I came out here to sit on the porch. But Lord knows He's made me happy as sunshine that you were the one He brought."

"I can smell dinner from here," Rose said, returning a tap to her mamaw's cushy behind as they walked toward the screen door that still had the same fist-size hole in it. Rose stopped to examine it. "Mamaw, why haven't you ever fixed that hole from when Christopher threw the ball through it?"

Mamaw looked down at the hole and tilted her head to ponder. "That there, Rosey, is a treasure of my grandba-bies. I don't have any plans for patching treasures. I only cherish treasures. And every time I look at that hole, I see my Christopher."

"And every time Christopher sees that hole, he remembers the switch he had to pull off the tree for his own behind to be whipped." Rose nudged her.

"And he turned out to be a wonderful boy, didn't he, now?" she said with a sly smile of her own.

Inside the kitchen, the table was set the same way it had been for all of Rose's growing up. Every serving dish from Mamaw's china collection held something, and steam was rising from each one. "All this for two people?" Rose asked.

"No, like your granddaddy told you, I had a feeling someone was coming by today. Now, sit, baby girl. Sit down here and tell us everything that is going on in your world."

They all sat down in the familiar golden vinyl chairs and held out their hands. Rose looked at the two precious, wrinkled, loving hands reaching out to hold hers to give thanks for the meal they were about to receive, and she felt ashamed and angry and all the things she didn't want to feel when about to give thanks with her grandparents. But she took each of their hands in her own and squeezed them. As if their hearts could in some way purify her own.

"Would you return thanks?" her granddaddy asked. Rose bowed her head, waiting for her mamaw to pray. Nothing was said for a few moments. Rose peeked with one eye, like she used to do when she was little, and she saw a small tear trickle down the cheek of her mamaw. The additional wrinkles on her face showed how she had aged since Rose had seen her last. They had both always looked old to her, but now, here, she really saw it. And her heart ached.

"Dear Lord, how can we thank You today for bringing our Rosey home to us? We knew You had something special planned today, but You've gone and surprised us good. And for that we are so grateful. Bless our sweet baby girl, and make her wise, and careful, and obedient. And Lord, . . ." Rose heard the slight waver in her mamaw's voice. "Don't let her be fooled by what life calls happiness, but let her long for the real life that You bring."

Rose felt a tugging inside of her. She knew happiness. When she was younger. When obeying and praying and all of those things were a part of her life. But she had grown so past all of that now. That silliness. That foolishness. Yet still she felt the same tug. And listening to the words of her mamaw, she heard no foolishness or silliness. A burning sensation crept its way through Rose's being and reminded her again, as it had multiple times over the last year, that there was still a desire inside of her heart for something. Anything.

"And bless this food that we are about to receive, and bless the loving hands of my sweet husband, who planted most of it, and You who made it grow. In Your precious name, amen."

"Amen," Granddaddy responded.

Rose just nodded her head.

"Take you one, baby girl," her mamaw said and slapped the largest fried pork chop on Rose's plate you'd ever want to see. Rose had yet to break the news that she was a vegetarian. So she always just cut up the meat, swirled it around, and ate the vegetables.

A pound of mashed potatoes were heaped on her plate next. They were followed by collard greens. "Jenny and I used to have a friend in school whose name was Corliss Green," Rose said. "But Jenny and I always called her Collard Greens."

They all laughed together.

"How's our Jack, Red? Didn't he want to come with you?" her granddaddy asked.

Rose felt the bite of mashed potatoes expand in her mouth even as she chewed. She swallowed hard. "Jack's been pretty busy lately. His job with the State Department is demanding—"

"Well, the two of you are going to have to slow up at some point and have children," Mamaw interrupted.

Rose set her fork down and looked wearily at her plate. She had fought so many battles lately. She didn't have the strength for any more. So she just asked quietly, "What's wrong if people don't want children, Mamaw? Would that be an awful thing for someone?"

The full, round face of Mamaw searched Rose's eyes for a moment. "You're asking a woman who birthed nine babies," she chuckled, then wiped her mouth. She placed her napkin back across her round legs. "I guess everyone has the right to do what they want; all I know is the treasure children are. And then the treasures they produce." She reached over and squeezed Rose's hand. "There's nothing like them. It's like having your heart outside of your body. You see your meanness and your kindness, and you see them grow up and become something, and then come home and see you again, and it's a love, baby girl, like nothing else I've ever experienced."

Her granddaddy took a swig of his sweet tea. "And if I'm not mistaken, Red, I thought it was your love for children that caused you to take this job of yours so far away from us."

Rose studied his face and shifted in her seat. "I do love children . . . just not sure I want any of my own."

"I love the way babies smell," Mamaw added.

Her sweet expression made Rose smile. Her mamaw noticed her gaze and lightly patted the top of her hand.

"How have you and Granddaddy loved each other for so long?" Rose asked, missing Mamaw's touch the minute she removed her hand.

"I just turn my hearing aid off," her granddaddy said, snickering.

Mamaw swatted at him, but a smile lit her face. Then she took her fork and scooped up a large wad of collard greens. "Daddy, you do not. Now, tell this baby girl why you've loved me for over fifty years."

"Because I do everything she says. What is that old saying? 'Happy wife, happy life'?"

Rose giggled. "Yeah, that's probably true."

He took another sip of his sweet tea, then held up the glass. "It's kind of like this mason jar," he began.

"Like a mason jar, huh? How's that?" Rose asked after savoring another bite of her potatoes.

"Well, see, Mama has the most beautiful crystal glasses that y'all are drinking out of. But she knows I like to drink out of this here mason jar. So even though she would prefer me to drink from her nice crystal, she still always puts out my mason jar. Why? Because she knows what it means to me. She knows it means that she loves me and wants me to be happy, even if she wouldn't necessarily do it this way herself," he said, giving his bride of over fifty-five years a wink.

Mamaw blushed.

Rose watched their interchange with wonder.

"And we're always honest," he said. He put down the jar, leaning back in his chair, and snapped his suspenders before continuing. "Never have any lies. Never have any secrets. Always tell each other what we feel, even if it means an argument or two. No argument hurt anybody. It's the silence and the secrets that will do you in."

Rose shifted her gaze to her plate and moved the collard greens around with her fork.

"What does Jack like?" her mamaw asked.

Rose lifted her head sharply. "What?"

"I said, what does Jack like? What makes him happy?"

Rose wasn't sure if her expression revealed her ignorance. She'd never really thought about what Jack liked. At least not that she could remember. And now they were such different people that she had no idea what he liked at all. "He likes music," Rose said, trying to offer an answer and remove the pause that could reveal the real reason Jack wasn't here. But she did at least know he was always listening to music.

"Okay, so Jack likes music. What kind of music? Country? Jazz? Rock and roll?" Mamaw did a little jig as she got up and headed to the kitchen. Rose and her granddaddy laughed as she returned to the table, carrying a chocolate pie topped with absolutely pristine meringue.

"So what kind, Rosey?"

Rose's smile faded. She stared at her mamaw with utter sorrow, her hands dropping to her sides. "I have no idea, Mamaw. I have no idea what kind of music Jack likes."

Mamaw sat back down and began to cut a piece for each of them, speaking to Rose matter-of-factly. "Then I'd say you need to go home and find out what kind of music Jack likes." She set the perfect piece of chocolate pie down in front of Rose.

Rose stared at the pie and ached at the thought of going back. Because as strong as the world thought she was, she wasn't strong enough for that.

Her grandparents hounded her no more. They just let her be their baby girl for the next two days. They fed her like she hadn't eaten in years. They watched *The Price Is Right* in the morning and *Jeopardy* in the evening. And in the afternoons she and her granddaddy would sit on the front porch and talk about the good old days, when Scout was still around, while they played checkers and *Aggravation* until their fingers were sore. The laughter those two days brought would have been enjoyed even more had Jack not called her multiple times. She had answered two of his calls briefly, and the rest she had simply ignored. She wasn't sure if she even cared what music he liked. Because that meant closeness, and closeness meant intimacy, and intimacy just meant more questions.

Rose woke up on her final morning to the sound of rain tapping on the roof. She had always loved that sound. She pulled the covers up around her and wished for life as she had known it. Because every time she came back here, that is how it felt. That life had returned to what it once was. Yet in her mind she knew that her life would never be as it once was, because another life waited for her beyond the reaches of the clapboard siding and tin roof that now surrounded her.

She could hear her mamaw scurrying about in the kitchen. The clanging of her cast-iron skillet and the smell of coffee infiltrated the atmosphere. Rose climbed out of bed and slipped on her robe. As she walked into the family room, she saw the back of her granddaddy's head through the window. He was in his usual spot on the front porch, rocking gently.

She walked outside. The warm South Carolina humidity could still be felt even through the falling rain. She breathed in the moist, warm air as if it were every beautiful smell of her once-known life that she so desperately wanted to capture.

"Will those legs still hold up this big girl?" she asked her granddaddy, knowing he hadn't rocked her in a long time. And this time was very different from those before. Because now she had committed all three sins the preacher warned against—she had lied, she had smoked, and she'd discovered what an adulteress was too.

"These legs will always hold up my Red," he said, holding out his arms.

Rose sat down gently and swung her legs across his as she had when she was little. She laid her head down on his shoulder and instinctively reached around his face. She took his soft earlobe between her fingers and rubbed it gently.

"You going to see your daddy while you're here?" he asked.

His words fell like a weight on her chest. "I don't go by there anymore, Granddaddy."

"Well, that's okay. He's not there anyway. That's just where his old earthly body is. He's already up in heaven, probably playing checkers with Jesus."

Rose felt tears come, burning with anger. "It should be my mother there and not him," Rose spat.

Her granddaddy's tone never changed. Even though she was talking about his own daughter. "One day you're going to have to quit blaming your mother, Red. She's suffered enough, and your anger doesn't make the outcome any different."

"Well, it makes me feel better," she assured him.

His belly shook. "Yeah, I can tell that it does." He sat there and rocked her gently for awhile, squeezing tight. She soaked in his love and protection, and they rested there, rocking silently until Mamaw called them in for breakfast and one last piece of chocolate pie for the road. Pie had milk in it, so Mamaw considered that good enough for breakfast.

———

The crashing dishes brought Rose back into the walls of the diner. She looked down at the chocolate pie still uneaten in front of her. She couldn't eat it. It reminded her of too much. And she had had all she could take of these memories and these tears and these emotions. She grabbed her purse and got up from the booth, pulling her shawl tighter. She pulled thirty dollars from her wallet and set it on the table.

Daisy came toward Rose as she hurried for the door. "Thank you for lunch," Rose managed.

"And for the fried chicken?" Daisy reminded.

Rose eyed her. "Sure. And for the fried chicken." She couldn't get through the glass door fast enough and was thankful for the cold wind that buffeted her as she exited. It reminded her of what her life was really like. Cold and harsh and hers. It was what she knew and how she was going to live it. No matter what any memory or crazy waitress had to say about it.

～

Daisy and Delores watched through the slats of the mini blinds as the striking and tormented redhead climbed into her expensive car. They left all of their customers and walked into the kitchen.

"Where are they headed?" the new cook asked the older gentleman who owned the place.

"Oh, they do this every now and then. They'll be back in a minute." He turned his attention back to the two disappearing beauty-store blondes and hollered, "And that's all you've got, girls, is one minute!"

Daisy and Delores closed the door of the small but neatly organized office in the back of the kitchen behind them, paying him no attention. They lit a small candle that Delores had on top of the file cabinet next to a hand-tiled cross her daughter had bought her one year for Christmas. Then they knelt down beside the worn leather office chair and held hands. They had both had a feeling all day that someone special was coming their way. And now that she was gone, they knew why. She was a hard one. With a big wall. They had torn out a few bricks with the fried chicken, but there was a lot more work to do. They prayed that whatever had been started in Rose's life today, God would send in someone, anyone, to finish it.

13

Rose started the engine and drove out of the parking lot, spewing gravel from her tires. She turned up the heat to full blast, the seat heater to the high position. But none of it was able to remove the chill that lived inside Rose's soul. Since she couldn't get rid of it, she wanted it to become her welcomed companion. Because if she could welcome it, she could find peace with it all somehow. She had learned ages ago that a person isn't willing to get rid of what she is willing to live with. And she had lived with these demons for so long now that she just wanted them to quit tormenting her and become part of her.

But something inside still resisted them. Something in her soul that wanted something more. Yet that same wanting was what had led to the dark places where she now found herself.

And here a waitress at a diner was trying to make her forget all that she was determined to be with a plate of fried chicken and a piece of chocolate pie.

"Well, it will take more than that," she declared to her empty car.

Her BlackBerry beeped, indicating that a new message had arrived. She picked it up and saw that she had ten messages. She couldn't believe she had spent that entire lunch doing absolutely no work.

"I am losing my mind," she confirmed to herself. "Helen will now officially know it is true."

The phone rang. It was Helen. She sent her straight to voice mail.

She couldn't stop again just yet, or she wouldn't make it home until tomorrow. She'd make sure at the next gas fill-up to read through them quickly and respond even more quickly. If she didn't think she would get pulled over again, she'd just read them and drive at the same time, but she resisted the urge.

The phone rang again.

"I'm not answering, Helen," she announced to the car. But when she looked at the caller ID, her heart officially stopped. It was Jack. She and Jack hadn't talked in almost a month. In fact, they hadn't talked since the day he left. The day he found out about Richard.

The phone rang again.

Her heart started pounding hard in her chest. Racing, in fact. What could he want? They didn't have anything to say to each other.

It rang again.

She stared at it while still trying to watch the road. "What would I say?" she asked the bright screen blaring his name at her from the dashboard. "Worse yet, what would you say?"

The name and number vanished from the screen. Her pulse slowed. Her mind, however, was another story.

———

The parking garage was dark as her high heels tapped the concrete floor. Her day had been busy, and seeing Richard tonight had helped her unwind. For the moment anyway. But she had to leave. She never liked staying overnight. Not since she had awakened there the first time. Plus, her absence would create far too many questions for Jack. They were dealing with enough issues to add this suspicion to the list.

The sight of a figure leaning against the passenger side of her car, facing her direction, startled her from her thoughts. She slowed her stride, panicking. For a moment she considered racing back to the elevator. But then she realized the figure was Jack. His ankles were crossed, as well as his arms, and in that moment she knew there was nothing she could say that would undo what this moment had revealed.

Rose slowed even more. Anger began to churn inside her, pushing toward the surface. As the anger grew, she steadied her pace and proceeded as if she were in complete control of this situation. She walked right past him and reached for the handle of the driver's door, which unlocked at her touch.

Jack turned around, and they stared at each other over the top of the car. Her expression conveyed disillusioned disdain. His, despair.

"You have absolutely nothing to say?" he asked, placing his palms firmly on top of the car.

"I think me being here and you being here says it all." Rose opened the door and tossed her handbag inside. "How did you find me, anyway? What did you do, use all of your buddies at the State Department to get the dirt on your wife?"

He offered a mocking laugh. "Finding you wasn't difficult. You've made little effort to hide your activities. In fact, the day you forgot your cell phone at home and this man's number came up five times in a two-hour period, I had a pretty good idea. But when I answered and the first words out of his mouth were 'I miss you,' I was pretty certain."

That remark stunned her. She thought she had been pretty conscientious in hiding her undertakings. Plus, Richard had never mentioned anything about it. But that was something she couldn't deal with now. "Well, however you found out, this really is none of your business."

His eyes registered shock, and he strode to her side of the car. "I can't believe you're saying this. In case you've forgotten, Rosey, you are still my wife."

"Well, I'm sure that will all be over with now," she said, challenging him with her gaze. Forcing him to make a move. She refused to flinch. Flinching would reveal emotion. She was all out of emotion.

"What did I do? Just answer me that, Rosey. What did I do to make you feel like you needed another man? Huh?" He was shouting now.

"This has nothing to do with you," she said, turning to lower herself into the car.

He grabbed her arm and pulled her upright, making her face him. "This has everything to do with me. And everything to do with you. And everything to do with our lives. I have been nothing but loving and kind. Even after your deception last year, I stayed with you. Trying to figure out what we could do to make this work. To get rid of whatever this stuff is that you're so afraid of. And this is what you do? You abuse my love for you? Is that all I'm worth to you?"

She stared at him blankly while a war raged inside her. One side wanted the life she had dreamed of, planned for. The other side wanted this man in front of her to understand that she couldn't be all those things he wanted her to be. That if he would just let her go, then he could go find what he deserved.

She pulled her arm from his grip.

"So that's your answer? No answer at all!" he said, running his hands through his tousled brown hair. "I just can't believe this. I can't believe you just spit in the face of nine years of marriage as if I'm not even worth an explanation. Well then, as you like it, Rosey." He threw his hands up in the air.

She remained silent. She didn't know what to say.

"I'll come by the house and get my things while you're at work tomorrow. That will remedy us having to have any more conversation, since you obviously refuse to even acknowledge what is really going on here."

"You have no idea, do you?" Her words came as a surprise to her.

"No, Rosey! I have trouble understanding insanity!" he replied, voice cracking. She saw him try to fight his tears and fail.

"Oh, so now I'm insane?" she spewed. "You're the one who has to have a perfect wife and perfect marriage and perfect family."

"I never asked for perfection, baby, just honesty."

"Well, your honesty meant it had to be your way!" she screamed, her voice reverberating through the layers of concrete and cars.

He took her arms again. "No, it didn't!" he shouted. "I just wanted you to tell me the truth!"

She felt a burning rise up her nasal cavities and fill her eyes. She fought those tears as hard as she had fought anything. "You can't deal with my truth, Jack."

He tried to pull her closer to him. She remained rigid. "You never let me try, Rosey," he said softly. "You never let me in close enough or deep enough to know what was going on inside you. All you let me see was what you wanted me to see. And I don't know what to do with make-believe. I only know what to do with reality. And right now, reality is a really bad place."

She lowered her head to avoid his stare.

He raised her chin, forcing her to look directly at him. He coaxed, "We're in a really bad place, but it can be fixed. This isn't an impossible place."

She looked at him in bewilderment and squirmed out of his hold. "I'm having an affair, Jack! You're standing here in the parking garage of another man's home, and I've just been upstairs with him. If that's not an impossible place for two people, then you are the one living in the land of illusion."

She saw the stabbing pain in his eyes and wanted to stop herself, but she felt the dam inside burst. There was no stopping what he had just unplugged.

"You want truth!" she screamed into his face. "I'll give you truth! I don't love you!"

"That's not truth," he said, and the calmness that settled over him made her seethe.

"Like I said, it always has to be your way. And if you don't like it your way, then you'll just try to convince people how it should be."

"Twist it however you want, Rosey. But you know that you do love me. And you can't handle it, because to stay with me means you'll have to deal with your demons."

She couldn't speak. She wanted to scream and tear her hair out or break something. Her gut felt as if those very demons Jack wanted her to get rid of had turned on each other and were now digging their way farther into her. Trying to carve out a safer place. The truth that was being spoken had stirred them. But they didn't want out. So they dug in harder. Farther.

She wanted to cry out. But she knew one cry, one ounce of need from her would be all Jack would need to stay. And he couldn't stay. And she would never act the way her mother had acted. She wouldn't beg. She wouldn't apologize. Because she had never burned Jack's dinner. And someone leaves because the other person burned his dinner, the ultimate revelation of no regard. Jack simply didn't understand her. She had done the best she could, yet he still couldn't understand her. Insanity, he had called it.

She regained her composure. "I've got nothing left to say, Jack." She turned and lowered herself down into the seat. He didn't try to stop her.

"This isn't what you want, baby. If I know anything, I know that," he said. From the corner of her eye, she saw his arms hanging helplessly at his sides. How did he seem to know that this affair wasn't about love but about comfort, that it was about intimacy without intimacy? Just the way she liked it.

She reached for the handle of the car door. "Then you don't know me." And with those words she slammed the door shut in his face.

She threw the gearshift into reverse, then punched the accelerator, letting her tires scream. Jack just stood there. As she peeled away, she glimpsed his face in her rearview mirror. By the time her car burst from the parking garage into the evening traffic, she couldn't stop the pain. And she knew she'd never forget that look. Jack's look. The look that broke her heart into just another piece. And all the king's horses and all the king's men could never put such a broken mess back together again.

⸻

The stranger with his Burberry overnight bag noticed the young man standing at the hotel-room door next to him. The man looked troubled and weary. If he wasn't mistaken, the man had even wiped away a tear with the back of one hand while fumbling to insert his plastic key into the slot. The man had no luggage, so the stranger thought maybe he had checked in earlier.

The stranger entered his own room, set down his Razr cell phone, and removed the diamond cuff links he bought in Europe on a recent getaway trip he and his wife of twenty years took just because. After preparing for bed, he called her and told her and the kids good night, but sleep was not to be found. The stranger heard loud cries and mentions of God and Rosey from next door. The man seemed to be fighting some kind of war. And there in the middle of the night, staring at the hotel-room ceiling, the stranger prayed. He didn't know any details, but he figured someone needed to be fighting this war alongside the desperate young man next door.

14

After Rose exited the parking garage, she turned the radio up as loud as she could to drown out the screaming in her head. She went home and took a shower, and scrubbed and scrubbed and scrubbed. She stayed under the water for almost an hour, certain that Jack would come home. He wouldn't leave. Not Jack. He was dependable. That was one reason she had fallen in love with him.

Finally, when her fingers had shriveled up to the land of unrecognizable, she got out. Standing in front of the mirror with a cream-colored cotton towel wrapped around her and her hair dripping wet, she simply stood there, staring at her reflection. She looked like a stranger. The dark brown circles under her eyes were competing with the brown of her eyes. And her skin didn't have the glow that she enjoyed when she actually found time to be outside, enjoying the sun and, come to think of it, enjoying life.

She lifted the handle of the oil-rubbed bronze faucet. Water rushed from the faucet, and she laid her washcloth in its flow. Everything moved as if in slow motion. Every action and every thought ran through her and out of her as if someone else were living her life. As she watched the water saturate the washcloth, she remembered when she had felt this way before. When there was death. This was the way she felt the day her dad died.

Rose slammed her hand on the handle of the faucet, and the flow abruptly stopped. With the slamming of her hand came a guttural yell. A wailing from the deepest part of her. A wailing that made mothers' hearts break and heaven's ear quicken. She fell down onto her knees, clutching her towel. Then she curled up on the brown marble floor and rocked. She tried to rock herself like her daddy had rocked her and like her granddaddy had rocked her. And as she rocked, she screamed.

Sometime in the early hours of the morning, Rose woke up cold and naked and alone. And still on the marble floor. She gathered her towel around her and dragged herself into the dark bedroom. She opened the bottom drawer of the dresser and put on some pajamas and crawled into the bed. She clasped a pillow tightly to her chest, and when she awoke to the sunrise, the events of the previous evening bombarded her as if they were fresh and new.

After getting out of bed, she walked into the closet and slipped into a green silk camisole and her black Ralph Lauren suit, allowing the lace to peek from the open buttons at the bottom of the coat. A suit that would say to the world that she was still in as much control as she had been the day before. But when she stood at the mirror, examining her diamond cross necklace, the last gift from her father, the one she had unwrapped the Christmas he had died, she knew nothing was okay. That everything was broken and disgusting and so not the plan. She put on her diamond floral earrings and Raymond Weil watch. And then she looked at the diamond platinum wedding band that Jack had given her.

She turned it slowly around and around. And then she pulled it off and laid it on the stone vanity. He would come by to get his stuff today. So she placed it in perfect view. He would never know she had shed a tear. No one would ever know she had shed a tear. But those tears would haunt Rose until . . . until . . . well, until she was willing to deal with them.

———

Brake lights in front of her brought her speed and her memory to an abrupt halt. In the short time since Rose left the diner, the weather had turned gray and foggy. A sea of red taillights in the dreary mist was all she could see through her windshield. A semi shrieked to a halt beside her. She rolled down her passenger-side window and waved to get the driver's attention.

He rolled down his window in response, gasping first at the frigid blast, then smiling so big at the sight of her that his mustache spread from ear to ear. "Whadya need, pretty lady?" he asked through the wad of tobacco forming a lump in the side of his jaw.

Rose loosened her seat belt to scoot toward the passenger window and craned her neck, trying not to smile at the trucker's obvious admiration. "Do you know how long this traffic jam is, or the cause of it?"

"Haven't had a chance to find out. Hold on a minute and let me see what my buddies can tell me." He held a CB radio up to his mouth with a plaid-flannel-encased arm. "Ah, breaker 1-9 . . . I'm out here at exit 58 near Fayetteville, North Carolina, trying to get the reason for the holdup out here. Anyone got any information I could use?"

The gridlock kept them side by side with no effort. Rose could hear the muffled sound of a voice offering a response.

He leaned out of the window and spit. She jerked the steering wheel instinctively. He looked at her as if she were a loon. "Uh, well, pretty lady, looks like we've got a two- to three-hour wait from where we are. Another rig has turned over, blocking the interstate, and it takes awhile to get these big ol' things out of the way."

She threw her hands up in the air. "Of course. That's what this entire day has been like."

"Need any help finding an alternate route?" he asked with another huge grin.

She was certain he would've helped her get to the moon. "No, I'll just see what back roads I can pull up here," she said, pointing to her dashboard.

"Well, you want me to let you over so you can get off here at this exit?"

"That would be great," she said with a smile.

"Where you headed?"

She hadn't intended on small talk. "South Carolina. Listen, I really appreciate all your help." And with that she rolled up the window. She'd had enough interaction with strangers today to last her a lifetime. Besides, her neck was getting stiff.

He pulled forward a bit so he could give her a wink and a hearty wave.

She returned the wave only.

The cars in her lane moved forward enough to let her get in front of his truck. She drove on the shoulder for a hundred yards to get to the exit. When she got off, she pulled into a Wendy's parking lot, stopped, and logged in to her navigation system, giving the address of her mamaw's and asking for an alternate route using the back roads.

The system obliged.

It also tacked on an extra hour to her trip. She pulled onto the road. She'd better make a call.

"HELLO?"

She never understood why people answered the phone as a question. And she wasn't in the mood to talk to Aunt Norma. So she put on her best impersonation of a Southerner.

"Can I spake toe Charlett, plase?"

It worked. "CHARLOTTE, SOMEBODY'S ON THE PHONE FOR YOU, BABY."

Maybe there is a God, Rose consoled herself.

"Hey," came Charlotte's voice over the phone.

"Hey, it's me," Rose said.

"How in the world did Aunt Norma not know who you were?" she asked, amazement evident in her voice.

"I still have my ways."

"So what's up?"

"Well, there's a wreck on the interstate, so I'll have to take some back roads. I'd give you a time of when I was actually going to get there, but at the rate I'm going, I may not be there until Christmas."

"Well, I can assure you we cannot put this on hold until Christmas. I don't think Mamaw or Granddaddy would like that much."

"I was joking."

"I know. I was just making sure you knew this was something that doesn't necessarily wait for people."

"So has anyone else arrived?" Rose asked, enjoying the feel of the plush leather seat and staring out the window. She watched the wind sweep through barren branches and listened to the sound of her windshield wipers as they moved rhythmically across the glass.

"Well, a few neighbors have stopped by. This house is so loud, we could win a hog-calling contest, and we don't even have a hog." She cracked herself up with that one.

Rose laughed too.

"And Christopher's here now," Charlotte added.

"Yeah, I talked to him earlier."

"That lit your mother up like a Christmas tree."

Rose ran her hands across the leather steering wheel, studying her manicured nails as she did so. "It always has," she responded. "Well, I'll call you when I have a better idea of when I'll get there."

"Okay. My side, Rosey, we haven't talked this much in years." Charlotte paused. Rose wasn't sure why she didn't correct her. Then Charlotte said, "I've missed it. I've really missed it."

Rose felt the corners of her mouth turn up slightly. "Yeah, me too. Okay, so I'll call you later."

"You better."

Rose studied the directions of the navigation system and continued on the rural two-lane road. Her BlackBerry had beeped twice while she was on the phone. There were twelve messages now. Twelve messages Rose had yet to check. She let the falling rain remove her from the pressure of the blinking red light. Rain always took her to the same place.

They slipped out of the restaurant into the darkness and the falling rain. This man by her side was still new to her. She felt that even after three months of dating him, she still had so much to learn about him. And he was always enticing more and more out of her.

They stayed tucked up under the awning at the entrance. "Want to run to the car with me?" Jack asked.

She couldn't believe he was inviting her to get soaking wet. "It's pouring, Jack."

He wrapped his arm around her and pulled her close, whispering in her ear, "A little rain can't hurt us. It'll be fun."

She leaned back and studied the glint in his eyes. She looked down at her black pumps. She couldn't believe she was even contemplating this. But she had never minded playing in the rain when she was little. And something about Jack brought out those childhood places in her.

"I'll race you," he said, his beautiful teeth shining in the darkness.

"You're crazy."

"That's why you love me." He tugged.

She retreated. She had never said "love." Had thought about it a few times, but never said it.

"You're overthinking this one, Rosey. Just run."

And before she knew it, they were running and laughing

and screaming down the street through the rain. When they reached the car, there wasn't a dry spot on them. They stood beside the car, bent over with laughter and gasping for air.

The parking lot was virtually empty because of the late hour. Jack's bright eyes met hers. He held out his hand. She reached for it. "Dance with me, Rosey."

"You are truly insane, Jack. We're soaked. And this is a parking lot, for goodness' sake."

"I know you love to dance, Rosey. I see you every time the music comes on. You're just itching to dance. You must've been a little dancer when you were small." He pulled her toward him.

"We don't have music," she yelled through the pounding rain.

"I'll make the music," Jack said and began to hum in her ear. And there in the rain, they danced. He twirled her. He dipped her. He kissed her. And every movement reminded her of how she had always loved to dance. And every movement convinced her that maybe she did love this man in front of her.

When he ceased humming, he touched her ear again with his lips. "I love you, Rosey Lawson," he said. "And I'm going to be your last dancing partner."

She didn't respond. She just leaned her head back and let the rain fall on her face. And then she danced. Again.

15

The new route, taking Highway 701, which eventually led to Highway 76 and home, allowed Rose the pleasure of driving back roads. She had always enjoyed it when she was young. She'd roll down her windows and turn up her music and just let life be. Life hadn't "just been" for her in years. The world was certain that she had life by the tail. What they didn't know is that recently she felt more as if life had her by the tail. She watched as the little town of Garland came into view.

She always wondered as she looked at homes what went on inside of them. Was there yelling? Was there loving? Was there food, where families sat around tables and ate together? Did they know their grandparents, or were they like most people, who had no idea what the older generation was doing, let alone how they were living?

The four-way stop sign brought Rose to a halt. Two little girls bundled from head to toe, with nothing but their noses sticking out, held hands as they skipped across the street in front of her. One's nose was chocolate, and one's nose was vanilla, but the strands of hair sticking out of vanilla's pink, fuzzy hood were strawberry.

———～———

Rosey and Jenny burst out of the back door of Rosey's house. They had been playing baby dolls and driving Christopher and Bobby Dean crazy. Finally, the boys had chased them out.

Once they stopped to catch their breath, Rosey noticed that the smell of honeysuckle was so heavy she thought she might reach out and run her fingers through it.

Rosey's daddy, wearing khaki shorts and a T-shirt, was in the backyard. "Do I have something good planned for you ladies today," he said. He held something behind his back with effort.

"Ooh, I love 'prises, Misser Lawson," Jenny said, letting go of Rosey's hand and slapping hers together. "Oh, lemme guess! Lemme guess! I love to guess!"

He chuckled. "Okay, three guesses."

"A dog!" She clapped vehemently.

Rosey started doing a dance of her own, side to side, trying to get a glimpse. "Oh, let it be a doggy, Daddy. Please let it be a doggy!"

"No, you need to guess a little smaller than a dog," he said, shifting his weight so they couldn't get a peek at the tantalizing object.

"A frog?" Jenny asked, turning up her nose. That wasn't her idea of a surprise. Not Rosey's either.

He smiled at her. "No, I don't mean smaller that way. I just mean not such a big purchase. And it's not alive, if that helps."

Their faces lost their glimmer. "It's not alive?" Jenny's lips curved down.

"No, I'm sorry, Miss Jenny, but what I hold behind my back is not alive."

"Well, is it a doll maybe?" She cocked her head in hope.

"Actually, it's edible, and perfect for a day like today," he said, then displayed a huge watermelon.

Rosey's eyes grew big, and she saw that Jenny had frozen with awe. "Who cares about a dog when you've got a watermelon!" Rosey shouted to the sky.

Rosey's daddy took the watermelon and set it on a white garbage bag that he had stretched across the picnic table. He placed a slice of that big ol' watermelon on a plate for each of them and set it in front of them.

They dug in like ants to chocolate. And by the time they came up for air, pink watermelon juice covered all three of their T-shirts. But not a one of them cared.

"Ooh! Ooh! Misser Lawson, there's a yellow jacket on that watermelon," Jenny said, hopping up from her seat and pointing at the small intruder. The honeysuckle that ran along the back fence kept them nearby most of the summer.

Rosey's daddy shooed the yellow jacket away with a wave of his hand. Then he surveyed their damage. "Well, girls, I would say we were hungry. We ate a big ol' hunk, nearly half!"

"It was so good, Daddy," Rosey said, wiping her mouth with the back of her hand, despite the napkin that was beside her paper plate.

"How about you two go rinse off," her daddy said, sliding his legs out from underneath the picnic table.

"Aw, Daddy, I don't want to take a bath. The sun's still shining outside," Rosey said, slapping her head into her hands.

He stood up beside her, his tall and handsome frame towering over her. "Oh, my sweet girls, Daddy has a better idea than that." They watched him carefully as he walked over to the side of the house and retrieved the new green lawn sprinkler.

Rosey couldn't believe their luck. Getting chased out of the house was just about the best thing to happen to them. She and Jenny jumped up from the picnic table and ran for the sprinkler, dropping clothes as they went. By the time her daddy actually got the water flowing, they were dancing in their matching Minnie Mouse Underoos, squealing at the top of their lungs. Before long, the rest of the Disney cast had joined them—Charlotte, Bobby Dean, and Christopher. They ran through that sprinkler the rest of the afternoon. Lucky those yellow jackets were more fond of watermelon than wet Underoos.

———⌣———

The sound of a beeping horn caused Rose to realize she was still sitting at a stoplight. The phone rang. The screen told her it was Helen again.

"Oh my word." She felt her pulse race as she accelerated. "I still haven't looked at her e-mail. She'll think I've gone certifiable. Well, I just won't answer it."

The phone rang again.

"But if I don't answer it, she'll be certain I've lost my mind, not answering two calls in a row." She stared at the screen.

The phone rang again.

She pushed the *receive call* button on the steering wheel. "Helen."

"What's that new secretary's name? You know, the one who works for that man up the hall . . . you know. My word, I can't even remember his name either."

Rose exhaled.

"I tell you, my memory is going south as quick as my boobs. I've been thinking about getting them lifted, actually. What do you think?"

Rose laughed. "I think that sounds like a great idea."

"So you think I have saggy boobs?"

"Oh no, I thought you were talking about your memory." Rose snickered.

"Okay, smarty, so what do I need to do with that memo? And if you tell me you haven't read it, I'm putting out an APB or calling Jack or something. Because you are not well, and neither is anyone else with you on the roads."

"Have you called Jack already?"

Helen paused.

"Helen." Rose's tone changed to scolding.

Helen's tone changed too. To one that sounded just like that of a mother. "No, Rose, I haven't called Jack. But he needs to be called. Because I'm sure whatever this is, he needs to know about it. And you know what I mean."

Rose bristled. "My life is my life, Helen. No calling Jack, and I don't need to be judged."

"I'm not calling Jack, and I'm not judging; I'm informing. And despite the fact that I'm your secretary, I care about you two, you ornery little thing."

Rose softened. "I'm sorry. This has just been a day like few I've had in awhile, and every time I stop to actually sit down and read through my e-mails, something else happens." Rose was defending herself. Rose never defended herself.

"Are you all right? Because honestly, in the seven years we've worked together, I have never heard you like this or seen you do things like this." Helen's tone softened too.

"Yeah, it's just all that's going on right now. But don't

worry, I'll get it done and get you the information as soon as I can."

"Well, I won't bother you anymore."

She sensed Helen's frustration. "You don't bother me, Helen. I promise. I'll call you as soon as I stop."

"Well, don't rush. I'm going to go get a pickle anyway."

"A pickle?"

"Yeah. What? You think there's something wrong with a fifty-year-old woman wanting to eat a pickle? They're not just for pregnant women. Plus, I could be pregnant, you know . . . stranger things have happened."

Helen never said good-bye.

———— ～ ————

Rose pushed the button on the dashboard that held Richard's number in memory. It was number 9. Jack was number 1.

"Where are you?" came his rich voice over the line.

"Somewhere in the backwoods of North Carolina."

"How's the trip going?"

"Long." She didn't feel like talking. The trip was getting to her. "Listen, I just wanted you to know that I've gotten some information that we're about to lose some of our support. We can't afford for them to collapse under the weight of the health-care initiative. I mean, the bill they've put on the docket now isn't even going to pass the Senate anyway." Rose's volume was escalating, but she couldn't stop it. "So why should they let a perfectly good education bill be sent to Neverland because they want to win friends that aren't friends in the first place?"

"Are you all right, Rose?"

"Yes, Richard, I'm fine," she snapped, not so finely. "This is very important. I've worked very hard for children and teachers, and we can't let this fail now because we lose sight of the ball."

"No one's losing sight of the ball," he said, his voice perfectly calm. "I know who's wavering, and I know what is needed to get them back in focus. What I'm not sure is what in the world is going on with you. You seem so irritable."

That was it. "Don't call me irritable! I am not irritable! Why in the world does everyone on God's green earth think I'm irritable? I'm a professional, Richard. A professional who gets paid a lot of money to perform for her clients, and that is what our relationship is about. This education bill."

"Oh, it is. Our relationship is about a bill. Well, that's news to me. That's not what it's been about this past year. Or the impression your phone call left me with just a few hours ago. And I'm trying to do everything I can to get her out of the picture. I know that's frustrating to you now that your husband is out of your picture. But things don't always happen like we want them to."

"I'm not sure I've ever heard anything truer come from your lips," she quipped, staring at the blurring dotted yellow line on the pavement.

"Well, you just need to get back home. And get this trip behind you. Apparently there's more going on than you mentioned. But I'll still be here for a couple of days. And I'm perfectly happy with us, Rose, so I'm not going anywhere. Whether she's in the picture or not, I'm not going anywhere."

Of course he wasn't going anywhere whether his wife was or not. Richard had it all. The perfect hostess wife and the perfectly beautiful and powerful lover. What more could he want? Loathing rose up inside her. "This isn't about your wife, Richard," she spat into the phone. "And this isn't about us. This phone call was about children and teachers. A bill that we need to get passed. A bill that I've worked on tirelessly. And a bill that I expect to get passed, whether you help me or not. I'll be back Monday morning, and it won't be to vacation; it will be to do my job. I'll call you first thing, and I'll look forward to hearing what your weekend has accomplished."

She pushed the *end call* button on her steering wheel and tried to release the tension that had wrapped itself around her neck. She never would have spoken to any other senator that way if her life depended on it. Richard was no longer "any other" senator. But for some reason she felt as though her life did depend on it. And looking at these tiny, peaceful houses that passed her with their expansive yards and brown wooden fences, she wondered how her life had gotten so far away from where she had thought she would end up. So far that she was certain she could never find her way back home.

And there was something in her that despised Richard. Despised the fact that she felt she needed him. Needed his understanding, his companionship, his respect. And then, staring at the blacktop in front of her, she realized that she didn't actually possess one of those things from him. Not one of the things she needed from him did he actually offer. And if she had been truly listening during that very first encounter, she would have known.

When they reached the end of the hallway, Richard opened the ornate wooden door marked with the brass-plated number 528. Their drinks and dinner had led them to his place. The dark paneled wallpaper and dimly lit sconces that spanned the halls at predetermined increments created an ambiance of warmth. Rose shivered.

"You cold?" he asked, placing his hand on the small of her back.

She wrapped her hands around her shoulders. "Just a little chilled, I guess."

His condo was in one of the prime sections of George-town. A lot of senators and their families lived permanently in their home states but kept secondary residences here. Children or husbands or wives would come up on weekends, and sena-tors would go back to their states during recesses. No doubt that carried a significant influence on the adultery and divorce rate in DC. Rose stamped out the thought as quickly as it had come.

She stared at the opened door for a moment. She looked down and studied the threshold. She had a passing memory of the day Jack carried her across the threshold after their wedding. For a moment it seemed as if his arms were wrapped around her even now. Tightly. Tugging her. But she knew his discovery this morning and the battle that had ensued had changed the playing field. They could never go back there again.

She looked up into the deep blue eyes of Richard, and he smiled gently, showing he was mindful of her struggle. A struggle he had obviously already defeated. She could only hope it had been defeated because of her. Yet somewhere she wondered if he defeated his struggle whenever any Roses came around. She felt his hand still supporting her. No, she was certain this was just about the two of them. Two desperate people in need of something desperately. Or something they had convinced themselves they needed.

She stepped across.

The door closed behind her. "Can I take your coat, Rose?" he asked. "I'll get a fire going, and you can warm up."

She removed her brown cashmere coat and gave it to him. He walked ahead of her into the living room, where he laid it gently across the back of one of the olive green leather chairs that sat across from the fireplace. He took his own coat off and placed it on top of hers. She remained in the foyer and watched as he walked across the room to the stone mantel and removed a silver lighter from it. He stooped down and leaned into the fireplace.

In a few moments the fireplace came ablaze. Richard stood, put the lighter back on top of the mantel, and turned his attention to Rose.

For a long moment they stood there, two strangers, simply staring at each other. Rose wished she felt warmer. "Come over here and sit down," he said, walking around the leather chairs and taking her by the hand.

His hand felt so gentle. He grabbed a large throw from the end of the rich green and taupe striped chenille sofa and took it with them. He spread out the throw in front of the fireplace and helped Rose sit down. She rested her back against the ottoman coffee table that sat in the center of the room. He was so polished. So smooth. "Red or white wine?" he asked, kissing the top of her hand as she looked up at him. The warmth of that kiss caused her to shiver once again.

"Red, please." She smiled softly.

His absence seemed forever. She didn't want to be alone with her thoughts. She stared at the fire crackling softly, yet artificially, in front of her. That was how all this felt, somehow. Artificial. Not the realness and genuineness that she had felt with Jack. She knew Jack loved her. She just knew he couldn't forgive her. Even though every touch and emotion and word had said he could. She knew from experience that betrayal wasn't forgiven. So why torture herself? She wasn't going to be like her father and let Jack win. No, she would remain in charge of her life in every way.

A crystal glass holding red wine appeared suddenly in the air in front of her face. She took it from Richard's hand. "Thank you."

"My pleasure," he said. Richard had removed his suit jacket while he was in the kitchen and his tie sometime during their hours of work at the Capitol. "Don't you want to take your jacket off?" he asked, placing his glass of wine on the tray atop the ottoman.

"Sure," she said, letting him help her take off her jacket. He placed it carefully beside her coat, making sure not to wrinkle it. He ran his fingers over the orange flower on the lapel. She wondered what he was thinking.

Finally, he joined her in front of the fire, but before he picked up his glass of wine, he smoothly slipped off Rose's shoes. "Prada. Nice." He smiled.

She looked at them. Staring at them now, she wasn't sure why she had paid so much for a pair of shoes. "Thank you. They kill my feet."

He laughed. "Well then, let me make your feet feel better." He took one foot in his hands and rubbed it gently. She resisted the urge to relax, but the wine, the fire, the touch, all of it lessened her anxiety. She leaned into the ottoman. Then she closed her eyes, hoping maybe that would remove the events of the morning from her mind.

When Richard kissed her, she wasn't even sure where she was. She wasn't even sure who he was. In her mind sometimes she saw Jack. Yet when she woke up with the sun coming through the cracks in the drawn curtains, when she caught sight of Richard's face next to her by the still-smoldering fire, she knew that the previous night had not been with Jack. And that what happened had changed her and Jack in an even greater way than her earlier deception.

She crawled out of Richard's arms as quietly as she could. She took another blanket, which was draped over the opposite end of the sofa, and wrapped it around her exposed body, then went through the living room and down the hall into the kitchen. A large window spanned the wall of an adjoining breakfast room. The table, the chairs, the drapes—every detail screamed of the woman who belonged here. And her name wasn't Rose.

Framed photographs on the mantel of the fireplace in the kitchen showed faces of Richard and his wife and their children. Rose's face wasn't in any of the pictures. That was because Rose's face was in her own pictures. Her pictures with Jack. She peered out the window at the row of town houses across the quiet street, wondering if any women like herself were staring at her. Hating themselves. Hating their lives. Hating the fact that no one in the rest of the world would believe they hated anything. Because that's how in control they were.

Rose let her forehead fall against the cold windowpane and clutched the blanket tighter. The freezing temperatures outside maintained the piled snow on the grassy places between the sidewalk and street. She felt tears well up and wanted to catch them, but how do you catch what can't be caught? They dropped on her hand, on the blanket. Something in Richard's touch had felt practiced. Something in the way he knew exactly what to say and do made her feel he had done this before. Had he been as new at this as she, surely his touch would have been more awkward. More hesitant. But he had made everything perfect. As perfect as adultery can be, anyway.

She crept back into the living room, where he continued to sleep. Silently she dressed and let herself out. Each step was a reason why she would never do this again. Rose Fletcher wasn't a woman who sneaked around. She and Jack might be over, but this wasn't how she wanted to spend her life. And she held true to all her reasons. That is, until she saw Richard the next weekend, when they had to have another meeting with her boss, Max, to finish up lingering details. Each time, she convinced herself it would never happen again. And each time, she wished that Jack would come rescue her.

16

Richard's name lit up on Rose's dashboard twice. She didn't answer. Helen's once. She didn't answer that one either. What was the use? She focused on her environment, the small towns, red lights, and stop signs, as she meandered toward Mullins. The small downtown street in the current North Carolina town was similar to those in the area where she was headed. The storefronts lining the main street of White Lake were adorned with hand-painted lettering offering gifts and crafts, antiques, and ice cream. The fluorescent red Coca-Cola sign with the little glass bottle in the corner reminded her of the two Cokes Daisy had forced down her. This required another stop.

She parked in front of a neon sign declaring Fletcher's Drugstore with a burned-out *D*.

."Who would believe that?" She stared at the hanging sign reflecting her own last name back to her. She'd pay with cash to avoid questions. She didn't know whether any of Jack's family lived in this area, but she didn't feel like engaging in any more conversations with strangers.

She tried to scurry inside but was met at the door by a lady about her age with a little boy whose arm was in a sling. Rose opened the door for them and hurried in behind.

"Mama, I'm going to check out the candy," said the little fella, who reminded Rose of a younger Christopher as he bolted from his mother's arm.

"We're checking your pockets before you get out of here," she hollered back. "Hey, Clint," the lady said to the young man sitting behind the wood and glass counter. He was restocking the playing cards.

"Hey, Sherry. Don't worry about him. I made him work so hard to pay back what he stole last time, he wouldn't even let it cross his mind now," he said, sliding the wooden door on the back of the counter closed.

"Well, he's an ornery one," she assured him, heading to the back of the store.

He looked up from behind the counter and caught Rose's eye. "Need a bathroom?" he asked.

Her eyes widened in embarrassment. "That obvious?"

"Well, you're not from around here, because I know

everybody around here. So I figure you're lost or gotta go to the bathroom."

"I could indeed borrow your restroom, if you don't mind."

"Well, ma'am, we don't need you to borrow it. Just use it for as long as you need to. It's back there past the toilet paper."

"That's an obvious place." she mumbled to herself, trying not to break into a run.

The small bathroom smelled of Lysol and was stocked with every automotive magazine published in the last decade. Obviously Clint got most of his reading accomplished back here. Rose washed her hands, left the bathroom, and headed straight for the door.

"You ever tried one of these, miss?" The little boy held up a 100 Grand Bar, effectively stopping her.

She knelt down beside him. "Oh yeah," she said, touching the candy bar with her index finger. "That is actually my favorite candy bar."

"No way. You're joshing me."

She laughed at his animated features. "I promise. That is my very favorite. It has caramel and crispy rice, and chocolate. It's delicious." She scanned the shelves for other delicacies. "Ooh, I loved these too," she said, picking up a Fun Dip pack.

"Ooh, yeah. Those are *my* favorites," he said, plucking the candy from her hand and tucking it with all his other candy into the curve of his sling.

She grabbed a pack of Gobstoppers. "Ever had these?" she asked.

"Oh yeah." He snatched those too. "I got these after I saw that movie *Charlie and the Chocolate Factory*. I think Johnny Depp is really cool."

She smiled at him and wondered if he had ever seen the real one. Gene Wilder had been a master in the classic. She tapped his cast. "How'd you break that arm?"

"Oh, I just fell out of a tree," he said, raising the right side of his lip and nodding his head.

"A big tree?"

"Huge," he replied, clearly enjoying his audience.

"My brother broke his arm once."

"Really? Did he fall out of a tree too?"

"No, he fell off a ladder."

"Ooh, cool," he said, chomping a piece of gum she hoped he had come in with but wasn't about to ask. "How'd he fall off the ladder?"

For a moment Rose couldn't remember why Christopher was even on the ladder. But then it all came back. The hole in the screen door. The switch. The punishment. The ladder.

———〜———

"Bobby Dean, you've got to scoot over. You're not in the strike zone," Christopher said, standing on his makeshift pitcher's mound as Bobby Dean squatted several yards in front of him.

Bobby Dean slammed his fist into his catcher's mitt. "Quit your yapping and just throw the ball."

Rosey was on third base, wanting to come home.

Christopher wound up the next pitch. It came high and outside. So high it made its way to Mamaw's front porch. And so wide it made its way right through her screen door. All three players gasped and flung their hands over their mouths, just waiting. They didn't have long to wait.

In no time flat that screen door flew open and Mamaw burst out of it, spatula in her hand and orange and black apron wrapped around her lime green dress. It was a brilliant display of fireworks. "How many times have I told you boys to play ball farther over in the parking lot?"

"But, Mamaw, then they might break one of God's windows," Rosey offered.

"Well, Rosey, God's got a little more money than Mamaw. Now, boys, because you disobeyed me, go out there and pull a switch and bring it on in here to me." And the screen door closed. It seemed to close with an exceptionally loud bang; either that, or all of their senses had become increasingly sharpened.

Rosey hated it when Christopher got a spanking. It hurt her worse than it hurt him. But the look of fear on his and Bobby Dean's faces proved they weren't the strong ten-year-old men she had thought they were. Bobby Dean and Christopher shuffled to the almost-barren tree in the backyard. Rosey tried to brush off the bottom of her denim shorts, still caked with dust from her slide into second, then ran to her mamaw.

"Oh, Mamaw, please don't whip those boys," she said, dashing into the kitchen, her bare feet slapping the pine floors, then the kitchen linoleum. "They didn't mean it. They were just out there playing and laughing and thinking about how good God's been to them."

"Rosey Lawson, don't you bring God into this. He didn't have anything to do with those boys disobeying their mamaw." She turned her back on Rosey as she flipped the corn bread fritters that were frying in her cast-iron skillet.

Rosey ran around the dinner table in the middle of the kitchen and tugged at her mamaw's apron. Big tears fell from her eyes. "But surely, Mamaw, there's another way. Surely you can make them do something that doesn't mean they have to get a whippin'. Daddy takes a doll away from me. Take their gloves. Take their ball. But please, please, Mamaw"—she tugged harder—"please don't give them a whippin' today."

Mamaw and Rosey turned around at the sound of the screen door to behold the two dejected souls entering. There they stood, each with a glove hanging from one hand and a switch from the other.

Rosey cried out one more time. "PLEASE, MAMAW. PLEEEEEEEEEASE."

"Rosey, Rosey . . ." Mamaw said, leaning down to capture Rosey's attention. "Okay, baby girl . . . It's okay. Mamaw will show these boys mercy today, because of how you have pleaded for them."

Mamaw studied the two boys. Rosey noticed that the blood seemed to be flowing back into their faces at this revelation of deliverance. "You two don't ever need to forget this," Mamaw said. She wiped her hands on her apron. "No switches for you today, because of Rosey."

Mamaw put her arm around Rosey's shoulder and drew her close. She ran Rosey's ponytail through her hand. "But you two will have a punishment. You are to go get Granddaddy's ladder and clean those leaves out of the gutter. That will save him from having to do it."

The two boys ran to the trash can, threw away their rods of punishment, and darted back outside. Christopher looked back and gave Rosey a smile. Mamaw knelt down and wiped the tears from Rosey's face. "You okay, baby girl?"

Rosey flung her arms around her mamaw's neck. "Yes, Mamaw, yes. Thank you, thank you," she said into her ear.

"You're welcome, baby girl. You're welcome."

Rosey wriggled away and ran out onto the porch to see what help she could offer the two redeemed derelicts.

The leaves were protruding from the gutters all the way around the house. Rosey heard the clanging of the ladder and the grunts of the two boys before she saw them. When they came into view, they were tugging the metal monstrosity across the front yard. Their muscles were showing, the ones they liked to flex in the mirror for Rosey as if they were the next Mr. Olympia. They would even cut off the sleeves of their T-shirts at the shoulders in the obvious hope that the world would enjoy the view of their newfound manhood. But their bulges weren't proving much of a match for the ladder.

"What are you boys doing?" Rosey's daddy asked as he came out of the front door of the church.

"They're getting out of a whipping," Rosey said, running across the wooden planks and down the three small steps at the side and into her daddy's waiting arms.

He kissed her cheek, and they both turned to watch Christopher and Bobby Dean. "Have they been naughty boys, baby girl?"

"Well, not real naughty," Rosey explained. "Mamaw said they weren't obeying her, but actually Bobby Dean just wouldn't scoot over far enough to catch the ball. But I didn't want to see them get a whipping, Daddy, so I begged Mamaw to have mercy on them. She says cleaning those gutters is her mercy." She patted her daddy on the back.

He set her down on the pavement of the parking lot. "Let me help you fellas," he offered, walking over and lifting the ladder. Rosey was relieved when her daddy leaned it against the house and the clanging stopped.

"We got it, Dad," Christopher assured him.

"Okay, okay. You boys have at it," he said, rubbing the top of Christopher's head. He turned his attention back to Rosey.

"What are we going to do with you, little firecracker?" he asked, touching the new tear on the side of her red bandanna-style halter top. "You keep chasing after these boys, and look what happens!" Rosey could tell by his tone that he wasn't really angry. "Your mama and I are going to run up to the store to get some groceries," he added. "Want to come?"

"Nah, they might need my help around here," she said, surveying her workers, who were beginning their ascent up the ladder.

"Rosey, we got this covered," Bobby Dean assured her.

She wasn't convinced. So she didn't move.

"Well, come home for dinner. Your mama's cooking meat loaf tonight."

Rosey wrinkled her nose. She hated meat loaf. Especially her mama's. It always came out with the smell of fire. "Daddy, I want to eat with Mamaw. She's already got dinner almost ready."

He leaned down and looked into her eyes. She knew he was serious when he did that. "You be home by five. Your mama is cooking, and we're going to eat it."

"One day she's going to kill us," Rosey said, completely convinced of her evaluation.

Her daddy turned away quickly to hide a smile, then started walking toward home.

"Y'all better move that ladder!" Rosey warned, watching Christopher as he reached as far as he could. Bobby Dean had one foot propped on the edge of the ladder, which made it easier to chew his fingernails. He was about as worthless as a snow cone in winter.

He spit a nail out and hollered back, "He's got it, Rosey. Just leave him alone."

"I wasn't talking to you, Bobby Dean," she retorted.

The teetering of the ladder caught them all off guard. By the time the top of the ladder started heading sideways, Bobby Dean jerked it for all he was worth, but Christopher's weight was entirely too much for him to retrieve. Rosey watched it all in slow motion. The struggle. Christopher trying to grab the gutter, getting nothing but a handful of leaves, the leaning and slow topple of the ladder as the metal slid along the house, clanging all the way down.

Christopher's holler, Bobby Dean's grunt, and Rosey's scream—all got Mamaw and Granddaddy running out of the house and her daddy running back up the street as fast as they could. But it was too late to remedy the inevitable. Christopher fell sideways into the porch railing, which then catapulted him into the shrubbery. By the time Rosey got to him, the bottom part of his arm was angled not so prettily on the top part of his arm.

Mamaw reached him next, saying, "Oh, Jesus, Jesus, Jesus, help my boy, Lord. Don't let him be dead, sweet Jesus."

By the sound of his screams, Christopher had to be hoping for dead.

"He ain't dead, Mamaw!" Rosey confirmed. "He ain't dead!" No one corrected her English.

Their daddy lifted Christopher gently out of the bushes and carried him straight to Granddaddy's pickup truck. "Mace, you drive, and drive as fast as you can," he instructed.

Mamaw hurried the rest of them into the car, and they sped to the hospital in fast pursuit of Granddaddy's pickup truck. By the time they made it to the hospital, Christopher and Daddy were in the back with the doctor. A nurse took Mama immediately to be with them. And there Rosey sat, with Mamaw and Granddaddy and Bobby Dean, knowing this was all her fault.

When her parents made their way back to the waiting room, they informed the weary waiters that Christopher was going to have to be in the hospital for three weeks with his arm in traction over his head. The doctor said his arm might never grow at the same rate as the other, so it could affect his ability to play ball in the future. And on top of it all, no kids under ten years old were allowed in his room.

Rosey started dying a slow death. She and Christopher had never been apart longer than a night for a sleepover. For three solid days she couldn't eat. She couldn't drink. Well, except Mamaw's half-frozen Cokes. On the third afternoon, after Rosey exited the school bus, she just meandered around the front yard, kicking at the ground with the toe of her sandals. She had been forced to wear shoes to school. She had protested. She hadn't won.

Her daddy appeared suddenly and guided her to the car.

"Where are we going, Daddy?" she asked, not caring very much.

"We're going someplace special, baby girl."

Even when he pulled into the hospital parking lot, Rosey didn't feel better. He sneaked her up a back set of stairs and right into Christopher's room. Christopher was lying flat, his head tilted up by a pillow, his arm in the air above him, with a stack of comic books beside him that their mama had brought him. The schoolbooks on the chair next to his bed looked neglected.

"Rosey!" he said when he saw her, his face lighting up.

Rosey ran to the side of the bed and grabbed his good hand. Tears started streaming down her face.

"Don't cry, Rosey. I'm going to be okay."

"But it's all my fault!" she wailed.

"Rosey, it's not your fault. It's my fault." He patted her hand, trying to console her. "Remember, you hollered at me not to lean over so far, and I didn't even listen to you."

"No, but if I had just let Mamaw give you a whipping, you wouldn't have ever been on the ladder in the first place."

Her daddy scooted another chair close to the bed, sat down, and pulled Rosey into his lap.

"Rosey," Christopher laughed. "It's okay, really. I would much rather be sitting here in this bed, not having to go to school, than having to get one of Mamaw's whippings."

She sniffled her snot. "Really?"

"Really. And look," he said, pointing toward the television hanging from the wall in front of the bed. "I can just lay here and watch TV all day!"

"That is so cool," she said, wiping her tears with the back of her hand.

"And watch this." He pressed a button.

Almost instantly a woman in a nurse's uniform appeared, sticking her head through the door. "Do you need something, Christopher?"

Rosey's eyes grew huge, and she peeked around her father at the nurse. Her daddy moved slightly to try to shield her from view.

"I was just wonderin'—," started Christopher.

"Wondering," their daddy corrected.

"—*wondering* if I could have some more of that red Jell-O when you bring me my lunch," he said, snickering quietly at Rosey.

She covered her mouth and snickered too.

"I'll see what I can do about that for you," the woman's soft voice responded. And her head was gone.

"See, Rosey? This place is the greatest. Though it's not Mamaw's food or nothin'."

"Anything," their daddy corrected again.

"Or anything, but it is pretty cool."

Rosey looked at his arm, fascinated by the contraption

holding it up in the air, and her face registered her concern. "Does your arm hurt?"

"A little sometimes. But they've got medicine for that." He shrugged his shoulders as if this place had the answer for everything.

Rosey leaned over and laid her head on his shoulder. "Well, I'm glad you're having fun and all, but I sure do miss you," she said.

Christopher tilted his head to kiss her temple. "I sure do miss you too, Rosey. But I'll be home soon, and you know what? I'm going to listen to you better when I get home too."

She popped her head up. "Really?"

"Yeah, really. I might even let you join the baseball team."

Rosey knew her face showed her approval.

When a nurse brought in lunch, she saw Rosey and gave her daddy a severe look. But before the nurse could say a word, Rosey and Daddy responded with their best pleading expressions. They worked. She relented and soon reappeared with one more container of cherry Jell-O.

———

Something tugged at Rose's sleeve. "Miss, miss! I said, did your brother's arm grow back okay?" asked the little boy in the drugstore aisle.

She smiled at his little face. "It grew perfectly," she confirmed. And it had. Even to the amazement of the doctors.

"Come on, little fella," the child's mother said as she headed toward them. "We've got to get home. They say we could get some freezing rain here shortly."

"Nice talking to you, lady." His small hand shot her a good-bye wave.

Rose was still kneeling down in front of the counter. She had blown most every rule she possessed today. And squatting there, staring at all of her favorite candy from her childhood, she decided she may as well just cross on over into the land of the absurd. She grabbed a 100 Grand Bar, some Gobstoppers, and a pack of Fun Dip. She had no idea how she'd eat that and drive, but maybe she could eat it in bed tonight while Charlotte caught her up on everything that she needed to be caught up on. She grabbed one more Fun Dip. Charlotte had loved them too.

Clint was behind the counter, picking a small piece of lint from his Tarheel sweatshirt. "Got everything you need, ma'am?"

She looked down at the pile and smiled. "I'm not sure *need* is the appropriate word."

He rang up the items. "Oh, everybody needs a little candy every once in awhile. That will be two dollars and forty-nine cents."

Rose reached into her wallet. There was no cash. She shifted her receipts around and checked between them. Not a piece of green to be found anywhere. She studied her credit cards. Surely there was one in there that didn't have the name

Fletcher on it. She pulled them out and fanned them, checking each name.

"Do you need me to spot you, ma'am?"

She laughed that embarrassed, "Don't be silly" laugh. "No, I just thought I had some cash. Well, I hate to use a credit card for this little amount. I'll just put it back," she said, reaching for the candy.

He placed his hand on top of the pile. "It's okay. People will come in here and spend a dollar and put it on their credit card. You look like you might need some candy today. Just give me whatever you've got."

Rose laid her Visa on the counter, hoping he wouldn't look too closely.

"Well, I'll be. Your name's Fletcher too?"

He was obviously thorough.

"Ah, it's actually my, um, my husband's last name."

"Your husband from around here?" he asked, now wearing a smile as though he'd just met family.

"No, he's from up north, actually."

"Oh, really? We've got some Fletchers up north."

"He's never mentioned relatives down south."

"Well, I bet you and I are related in some way. You give me your address, and next family reunion, I'm going to invite you and your husband—um, what did you say his name was?"

"I didn't."

Clint cocked his head at her.

True Southerners didn't do rude. She'd been gone for awhile. "It's, um, Jack."

Clint's head went back down. "Well, I'm going to invite you and Jack. Who knows, we all might be first cousins or something." Rose sighed heavily. Clint heard her. "Don't like family reunions?"

There was no need to bring this nice man in on the fact that she and Jack weren't celebrating anything together these days. "Actually, no. I'm just really late for where I'm headed."

"Oh, I'm so sorry, ma'am. I wasn't even paying attention. I hope I haven't kept you from something important. Well, you just sign right here," he said, pushing the receipt and a Coca-Cola pen toward her. "And we'll get you off and running. And I'll just need your address right here," he said, pointing to the bottom of the receipt.

She knew he didn't need her address; he just wanted her address, and she didn't give out her address. Not unless she was ordering something online. She wrote her address down. Not completely correct, but an address just the same.

"I hope you enjoy your candy, ma'am. And you tell your husband there are some Fletchers in North Carolina that are dying to meet him."

"I'll do that," she said as she opened the door and the bells jingled at her departure.

Clint watched the dignified woman as she climbed into her fancy luxury car. He looked at the address she had written on the slip of paper. He knew it wasn't the real one. He could tell by the way the pen hesitated as she wrote. Hesitation reveals multiple things.

He sat down in the chair behind the counter and rested his elbows on the glass, then leaned his head into his hands. For some reason he knew the Fletchers from up north were having a cold winter. He could see it by the distance in her eyes.

He looked at the small crucifix of Jesus and the rosary beads his grandmother had hung up next to the cash register. He kept them there because of what they meant to him. His grandmother had told him she had "run out of rosary beads" praying for him. It had worked.

So today he prayed silently but desperately that something about the warmth of the South would reach inside Rose Fletcher's heart and help her and Mr. Jack Fletcher have a wonderful Christmas. He prayed it would be the best they had ever known.

17

Rose had never quite figured out why people in the South were so nosy. It was one thing up north for your close friends to know your business, but another thing for strangers. They pretty much left you alone. She had grown fond of that. But down in the South, perfect strangers would grab you in the line at the restroom and ask, "Can I hug you?" if you even remotely reminded them of their dead Aunt Julia. And if you were pregnant, well, have mercy, your belly would be like a Magic 8-Ball.

But there was something about her life now. People gave her space. Let her breathe. Didn't really notice her in the bathroom lines. Unless they were from the South themselves and had been transplanted. And Rose could usually spot a Southerner a mile away. They always made eye contact, even in elevators.

Rose hooked her seat belt and backed out of the space slowly. She pulled back onto the main street. About the time she reached a long stretch of blacktop with no lights and just countryside, her e-mail beeped on her phone.

She cursed. "I can't believe I did that again," she told the hum of the heater. "There is not a living soul who would believe I've gone all day without checking my e-mail. I wouldn't even believe it if I weren't the one doing it." She picked up her phone and noticed she had also missed another call. It was Jack's number. Again.

"What could he want?" Her heart started hammering. "I'm not calling him. I'm not."

The ringing cell phone interrupted her musing. Christopher's name popped up on her dashboard panel.

"Hey." She tried to sound completely together.

"What's wrong?" It never worked with him.

"Jack just called. Again. He's called twice in the last hour, and I have no idea what he could want." Her thumbs tapped the steering wheel.

"Well, maybe he heard you were coming home, and he's calling just to check on you."

"But we haven't spoken in almost a month."

Christopher paused. "Then maybe it's time you did."

Rose puffed. "I am not calling Jack."

Christopher gave her time to soften. She did. "What would I say?" She paused. "No, that would be the most ludicrous thing I've done in, well, the last month." Her track record was growing shorter and shorter.

"I doubt you'd regret it."

"I'd love to change the subject."

He sighed. "All right. Let's talk about how much longer until you get here. Willie and Sharon just got here, and they were asking about you."

"You mean Shayrun," Rose corrected.

"I mean Sharon," he assured her.

Rose could have slapped herself. "You mean her name is spelled S-h-a-r-o-n?"

"Rosey, please tell me you didn't think her name was actually Shayrun."

He was the only living soul she would ever admit such error to. "Yes, my sweet brother. I have spent the last thirty-three years thinking her name was Shayrun."

He laughed. She couldn't help but laugh herself. "Oh my," he said. "I thought the North had wised you up."

"You obviously can't get the country completely out of the girl." She laughed again. "I'll be there in a couple more hours."

"Well, if I don't hear from you in a couple, I'll call you again. Because I hear there might be some freezing rain headed through here."

"I'll be fine. Trust me." Though the elements outside her car weren't looking so assuring.

"Sure, I'll trust a woman who doesn't know the difference

between Sharon and Shayrun." He was still laughing when he hung up.

Rose's mind felt at ease. For one moment her mind was actually at ease. Those moments were so rare to her, especially anymore. Lately she had been living her life trying to fix something or hide something or ignore something. Never just empty of something. But for one brief moment on that country stretch of blacktop in North Carolina, as the faded yellow center line blurred by, Rose had no somethings. But it only lasted a moment. Because then Jack came back. And he returned with a vengeance.

———

Rose had gotten up early that morning to work out. Finding the time had been almost impossible since her schedule had gotten so crazy. She'd been laboring to get new legislation ready to take to Congress, and that meant almost no free time. She and Jack used to work out together in the evenings after they both got off of work, but he was traveling more, and she was working later hours. So she took the opportunity whenever a morning allowed it.

She figured Jack would already be at work by the time she returned from the gym, but she came through the back door and found him sitting on the sofa with his back to her. He never turned around as she walked in behind him.

"I thought you'd be gone," she said, tossing her keys

onto the glass side table beside the sofa and heading to the bathroom.

She threw her gym bag down on the floor beside the large Jacuzzi tub and went into the closet to pick out her clothes for the day. She reached for her navy blue suit with the small white pinstripes and the white camisole. The new orange flower would be the perfect accent. She heard Jack's footsteps come into the bathroom. She turned in the closet so she could see him. He was leaning against the stone vanity. His expression granted an immediate revelation that something had happened. Something bad.

"Jack, what's—" Then she saw what he was holding. Her birth control pills. Obviously her hiding place wasn't as good a hiding place as she had thought. She couldn't breathe.

He stared at her, his blue eyes not even trying to conceal their hurt. They were so broken. She felt a twitching in her jaw as she steadied herself for what would ensue. "Where did you find those?" she asked.

"Is that what you're worried about?" he asked. "Where I found them? If that's your greatest worry, then I guess this really is as bad as I thought it was." He set the packet down on the counter. Rose looked at him there, in his jeans and black turtleneck. She wanted to tell him everything. Explain it all. But she couldn't. Pride was a powerful friend.

His tone was calm when he said, "So you've done nothing but make our life a game of charades for the past three years.

What else is a lie, Rosey? Our marriage? Has all of this been a charade to you?" She was amazed by how he contained his obvious passion and anger.

But she had to turn her back to him. To get away from the harsh reality of his gaze. At her movement, he lost patience with her. He grabbed her arm and spun her back around. "You will not ignore me this time. You owe me answers."

"I don't have answers!" she screamed, jerking her wrist from his grasp. "You always want answers. I don't have answers. I just know I don't want children, and all you've done since we've been married is hound me about children."

"That's not true, Rose, and you know it! We both wanted children when we got married. We talked about it and dreamed about it together. So if you changed your mind in the middle of the game, you should have let me know."

She felt like an exploding bomb. "You don't know me, Jack! You don't really know me! You have this idea of who I am, and you just believe what you want me to be. But that's not who I am. I'm none of those things you want me to be!" She was crying now, and she hated herself for it.

He took her trembling body into his arms. She fought him, raging and crying, with every ounce of her power, but he had handled stronger foes than Rose. His arms were like a vise. Finally, she gave up her struggle.

They both fell onto the floor of the closet. "I love you, Rosey," his voice whispered softly in her ear. "I love you with all my heart, and we can figure all of this out. I just need you to talk to me, baby. Just talk to me."

Rose let her body sink into this man. The man she loved. A man she had forced into becoming a stranger. Yet there was something undeniably familiar about this moment. He kissed her wet face. She felt so tired. All she truly longed to do was stay there in his arms on the floor for years and years and never leave.

But the battle inside never rested. Within minutes it had forced its way back to the surface. Rose leaned back and removed herself from Jack's arms. She got up from the floor of the closet and looked down at his face. "I don't want children, Jack. So if that ends this marriage, then that is just what will have to happen." She stripped off her clothes and stepped into the shower.

When she got out of the shower, Jack was gone.

A tear burned down Rose's cheek, leaving a trail of coolness. Her e-mail buzzed again. "Oh, I can't do this any longer. I've got to respond to these," she said, wiping her face with the back of her hand. She spotted a parking lot and pulled in to check her e-mails. She left the engine idling and the heat going to keep her warm. She didn't notice the Elizabethtown AME church sign.

A plump black hand shifted the black wooden plantation shutter slats to catch a clearer view of the new arrival. He saw the dark car parked in the lot and the red mane of hair dropped down either praying or looking for something. Pastor Lionel Johnson rubbed his blue cable-knit sweater where it bunched over his stomach. He was pretty certain this was the reason for the restlessness he'd been feeling all day.

18

It took Rose thirty minutes to answer all of her e-mails. Her fingers had grown so nimble on the small keyboard of her BlackBerry that she hardly even had to look at the letters anymore. Most of them were wearing off anyway. Finished, she laid the BlackBerry in the passenger seat and tilted her head back against the headrest.

Helen rang. Rose answered.

"I have officially called off the search committee," Helen informed.

"I'm very grateful."

"Have you ever noticed how Max hikes up his britches every time he gets frustrated?"

Rose moved her head from side to side, stretching her neck. "I can't say that I have."

"Well, I've been privileged to observe it close to fifteen times today. So I'm going home now. My brain is fried. My nerves are shattered."

"And I'll bet your little happy container is empty too."

Helen gasped. Then Rose could hear her drawer open and close. She knew Helen was checking to see if her flask was still there.

"You need to stop that."

"We all need to stop some things," Helen retorted.

"Touché. And good night."

"Be careful, sunshine. I'll talk to you tomorrow, I'm sure."

"I can hardly wait." Rose ended the call.

That was when Rose saw the church sign. And that was when she took notice of the small, white clapboard chapel with a red door and black shutters.

A Christmas wreath hung on the front door, and two tall holly trees stood at each corner of the building. It looked like a postcard. The interior shutters were all angled to match perfectly, except for a slight extra tilt in the one on the left front window. Rose put the car in drive and headed for the exit of the parking lot. But as committed as her car was to that direction, her heart was pulled to the opposite one. Something inside her desired just a few minutes inside the small chapel.

She debated with herself. An occurrence that was becoming more frequent. And the majority of this day, out loud. The stronger Rose usually won, but today the stronger Rose had been weakened. *Memories can do that to you.* She gave a loud sigh and turned the Lexus around, convincing herself this really was a good idea.

The shutter tilted back into place. But Rose never noticed as she stopped the car in the parking spot nearest the red door. The church was much different from the brick Church of God across from her mamaw and granddaddy's, with its white door and white shutters. But something about this church felt familiar. Inviting.

Rose pulled her wrap up from behind her and draped it around her shoulders. She cut the engine, got out, then dropped the car key into the pocket of her slacks. She locked the door with a push of the button on the door handle. Before she could change her mind, she climbed three concrete steps in front of the church and reached for the aged brass handle that led inside. The door swung open silently. *Good,* she thought. No announcement of her entrance.

In the small vestibule, she inhaled the tangy scent of pine. A Christmas tree with tiny lights illuminated the intimate area. She paused only for a moment, then entered the sanctuary, where soft lights added to the peaceful environment. Rich, dark pews padded in burgundy velvet were a deep contrast to the white walls and black interior plantation shutters. She aimed for the back pew, wishing she'd worn shoes that weren't so loud on the hardwood floor. She touched the dark grain of the pew, then decided she wanted to go closer to the front.

Rose hadn't been inside the walls of a church for years. Jack had started attending church shortly after their wedding. A colleague in his office had invited him, and he had gone ever since. He'd invited her to go with him, but when she refused, he went without her. But she had grown up inside church walls very much like these. Practically raised there. Falling asleep on pews. Even forgotten on them a time or two until her father returned to scoop her up and carry her home. She was always surprised that the aroma of fried chicken cooking next door hadn't instantly woken her up. The memories made her smile.

She sat down quietly in the fourth row and leaned back. She ran her hand across the soft but worn velvet beside her. And with the soft fabric beneath her hand, she remembered.

———

"You going with Mamaw tonight, Rosey?" Mamaw asked as Rosey stepped inside their house.

Her mama and daddy had already gone over to the church to rehearse with the choir. Her mama had dressed Rosey in her favorite sundress, orange with small ribbon ties on her shoulders. Mama had also pulled back Rosey's hair with an orange-ribboned headband. Rosey loved orange. "Yes, ma'am," she replied, letting her little purse dangle from her forearm. "I thought I'd go with you tonight."

Mamaw, Granddaddy, and Rosey walked together across the parking lot to the tiny brick church. She swung their hands as they walked, her purse flopping on her arm in rhythm. Rosey could hear her mama's organ playing before Deacon Wilson even opened the door to greet them. Granddaddy kissed Mamaw, patted Rosey on the head, and went to stand with the other deacons.

It was a Sunday evening service, and somewhere in the middle of the preacher's sermon, Rosey laid her head on her mamaw's lap. Something about the preaching always made her eyes heavy. Fortunately for her, at six years old she was still allowed to sleep in church. And Mamaw had a way of stroking her hair that just put her out quicker than the preacher could say, "And a . . ."

But something happened at the end of the message when sister Sugar Mae Jacobson got to the piano. The Spirit came down, and Rosey's mamaw caught ahold of Him. Rosey had heard people pray in the Spirit on a few occasions, but never a person in whose lap her head was resting. So when the Holy Ghost made its way to their pew and Mamaw started praying in the Spirit, a current swept through Rosey's entire body. It jolted her upright. Rosey wasn't necessarily scared. No, she was just mesmerized. She wasn't sure what was going on, but she knew Jesus had arrived on Dixon Street that evening.

Rosey sat quietly while her mamaw worshiped the Lord right there in their pew. Rosey watched Mamaw intently, remembering every moment. The raised hands, the falling tears, the faint but Holy Ghost–inspired prayers. Sugar Mae wept at the piano stool, and the pastor prayed over a couple at the altar. And in the middle of all the activity surrounding her, Rosey felt something deep and rich and warm inside her.

While the rest of the world was worshiping the Lord, with her mama on the organ and her daddy singing softly from one of the chairs on the platform, Rosey approached the kneeling bench at the altar. An elderly woman who smelled of peppermint and wore hats with flowers on them came and knelt beside her and prayed with her. And there, Rosey gave her heart to Jesus.

When Rosey got up from that bench, she knew that something important had happened inside her heart. Her mamaw was smiling at her as she returned to the pew. She wrapped her arms around Rosey in a big, cushy hug. And when she let Rosey go, Rosey saw Granddaddy in the back, drying his eyes with a handkerchief. When she pointed it out later, he told her it was just his eyes sweating.

Revival had come to that small country church on Dixon Street in Mullins, South Carolina. And Rosey got a little of that peace her mamaw always told her living for Jesus gave, the peace that passes all understanding. Right then Rosey felt that peace, then and ever after. Well, at least until her family moved away.

———〜———

"Lost in thought?" The booming voice reverberated through the empty church.

Rose stood up quickly. "Oh, excuse me . . . I'm so sorry . . . I was just . . ."

"Sit down, child. You don't have to be sorry for being in the house of God. That's why we keep the doors unlocked. You never know who might need to come inside for awhile."

Rose didn't sit.

"Sit. Please. I'd be upset if I disturbed you."

She sat back down slowly.

"Lionel Johnson," he said, extending his hand. "I'm the pastor here." A thin layer of gray fuzz covered his black head as though he had recently shaved.

"Rose Fletcher," she said, extending her own.

"Well, Rose, I'm glad you could stop by today," he said, sitting in the pew in front of her. It squeaked as his weight settled in. He twisted his body and put his arm on the back of the pew, a good position for chatting.

She didn't really feel like chatting.

"Where are you from?" he asked. "Your face doesn't look real familiar."

"Oh, I'm just passing through on my way to South Carolina," she said.

He scratched his head. "Where at in South Carolina?"

"Oh, I'm sure you've never heard of it. It's just a small country town named Mullins."

"Mullins! You've got to be kidding me." He slapped the back of the pew, knocking his gold wedding band loudly against it. "I've got a sister born and raised in Mullins. She lives in Florence now, though."

"Really?" Rose couldn't help but be intrigued.

"Yeah, her name's Gladys."

Rose's eyes widened. "Not Gladys Lewis."

"Yes! Gladys Lewis. That's my sister. She lived on Dixon Street."

Rose had trouble allowing this to register. "Does she have a daughter named Jenny?"

"Yes, and two boys." He smiled and leaned back. "Don't tell me you know them."

Rose laughed softly. "Jenny was my best friend growing up."

"Well, I'll be. You must be Rosey."

Rose stiffened. "It's Rose, actually."

"Well, Rose Actually"—he smiled—"Jenny talked about you all the time. In fact, she still talks about you every now and then." He slapped his knee and shook his head. "She will not believe this. I'm telling you, she will not believe this."

"I don't think I believe it."

"Have you and Jenny not kept in touch through the years?" He leaned back toward her.

"I haven't kept in touch with many people back home. Life where I come from has a way of consuming you." She looked down and ran her fingers along the edge of her wrap.

"Well, well, Jenny's friend Rosey, living and breathing right here in my church. Who would ever have imagined?" He chuckled, his belly shaking. "You wouldn't believe Jenny now."

Rose softened. "What's she doing?"

"She's been a nurse for about eleven years. Has three beautiful children. All boys. Darryl, Duane, and Allen, and they are live wires, let me tell ya! She and her husband live in Florence too. He was a pro football player, but now he's pastoring a church, and Gladys lives with them. Oh, Rosey . . ."

"Rose," she corrected, gently this time.

"Yes, I'm sorry, Rose. I know if she knew you were going to be this close, she would just love to see you."

It seemed like just yesterday that she last saw Jenny. Then again, it seemed like forever.

———~———

Jenny ran into Rosey's house and screeched to a stop because of the boxes that filled the family room. With Rosey sitting glumly on top of one.

Jenny retreated for a moment to set down her duffel bag and a can of mosquito repellent on the porch. "I can't believe you're leaving, Rosey."

"I know. It just sucks," Rosey replied bravely, knowing her parents were at her mamaw and granddaddy's.

"Yeah, it sucks cheese." That was Jenny's new favorite saying.

"We're staying at Mamaw's tonight, because Daddy already took down our beds."

Jenny stroked her chin. Rosey knew that meant she was thinking.

"What?" Rosey asked.

"I know!" Jenny shouted suddenly. "I say we camp out instead." Jenny pulled Rosey off the box and led her outside. "Look at this night. Just look! It's going to be perfect." Jenny grabbed the can of Off! and sprayed her arms with it, her mother's summer staple. The mosquitoes had been exceptionally pesky since summer had arrived, which meant Jenny always smelled of insecticide.

"Oh, that's a great idea, Jenny!" Excitement grew in Rosey. "Granddaddy's got a great tent, and we can set it right up in his backyard."

They sat on the steps, talking as the evening grew dark. Soon fireflies flickered and danced through the darkness. "Let's go get one of your mama's mason jars and catch us some of these fireflies," Jenny suggested.

"She'll whip our butts," Rosey replied, shaking her head. "You know those are for those tomatoes she was going to can."

"Your mama ain't never canned nothin'," Jenny reminded.

Rosey shook her head. "I know. It sounded crazy to me too."

"Well, you're moving anyway, so I don't think she's going to be needing them." Jenny could be pretty smart.

"Well, they're probably all packed up."

"Of course they're packed up, silly. She's never even opened them."

She had Rosey there. "But she'll know we've been in them."

"By the time she figures it out, she won't even remember why she got them in the first place. So come on, scaredy-cat. I'll get them out if you need me to."

Jenny grabbed her hand, and they ran back into the kitchen. The boxes were piled high, but it didn't take them long to figure out exactly which one held the mason jars. It was written all over the box. As if Jenny had taken to stealing on multiple occasions, she reached in, pulled a jar out, and left the box almost exactly as they had found it.

With a screwdriver from the toolbox in the garage, they poked holes in the lid. They tucked the jar safely inside Jenny's duffel bag that she'd brought so she could spend the night; then they went over to Mamaw and Granddaddy's, where Rosey's daddy and granddaddy were rocking on the front porch. The smell of fried catfish wafted through the air. Rosey's stomach rumbled.

Her daddy eyed them. "What trouble are you two barefoot travelers up to this evening?"

They looked at each other. "Ahh, nothing much," Rosey responded, walking over to the porch and sitting down on the middle step. Jenny plopped down beside her.

"Are you staying for dinner too?" he asked the duffel-bag carrier.

"Oh yes, sir. I'm staying for the whole night," she informed him.

He laughed. "Well, we're glad you can join us."

Rosey looked up at her father. "Daddy, we're wonderin'—"

"Wonder*ing*."

She placed her hand on her hip. "Dad . . ." She was eleven years old now. He shouldn't be reprimanding her. Especially in front of others.

Her granddaddy chuckled.

"We were wonder*ing* . . . if we could borrow Granddaddy's tent and sleep outside tonight. You know, kind of like we were camping."

Her granddaddy turned before her daddy could speak. "I'd love for you to borrow my tent," he said, leaning forward slowly and extracting himself from his chair. "You and Jenny do whatever it is you were doing, and we'll get the tent out for you," he said, punching his son-in-law on the arm.

"Girls, don't be gone too long, now. Dinner will be ready in about fifteen minutes," her father reminded.

They raced away. Rosey and Jenny shared a moment of relief that Rosey's daddy didn't notice them take the duffel along. By the time she and Jenny had successfully captured a small army of fireflies, their camp was sitting neatly, all set up in the backyard. Giddy with excitement, they unzipped their home for the evening. The scent of dinner surged toward them. Inside the tent they found two trays holding substantial plates of fried catfish, french fries, fried corn bread, and coleslaw. And beside each plate was a mason jar full of sweet tea.

They sat their own flickering jar down between the plates and took their places. "We've got ourselves a feast, sister."

"I'd say," Jenny said, licking her lips. "And our own firefly lamp."

"Well, I do believe you're right." And the two dined by a special kind of firelight. And sometime in the wee hours of the morning, after they had talked and laughed and cried over Rosey's departure, the last flickering tail went out.

19

"What are you doing on these back roads?" The pastor's loud voice brought her back.

"Oh, there was a bad wreck on the interstate," she said, straightening her wrap. "I used to travel two-lane roads like this all the time, though, back when I was in college. I always enjoyed the small towns I would drive through."

"The best place for boiled peanuts and Coca-Cola." He chuckled.

They shared a knowing smile. She glanced down at her watch. "Oh, mercy me," she said, startling herself. She had not just said "mercy me." She hadn't said "mercy me" in years. "Well, I'd better get back on the road, or they'll all think I was just pretending to come home." She stood up.

"I bet home will be excited to see you." He rose as well.

"Well . . ." She cleared her throat. "You have to do what you have to do."

"Well, we'd love for you to come see us again. Maybe in the summer, when it's a little warmer," he said as they made their way to the foyer. Rose looked at the Christmas tree again. She turned away from it, trying to turn from the memories it brought.

"I don't know when I'll be heading in this direction again," she said, ready to leave even more quickly now.

"Well, we have some mean covered-dish dinners in the summer, after church, if you're ever out this way again and hungry." He raised his bushy eyebrows up and down. Apparently the hair meant for his bald head had gotten stopped at his eyebrows.

She paused.

"I haven't been to a covered-dish dinner in ages. And, oh, Southerners love a good covered-dish dinner, don't they? It gives them a chance to show off. When I was growing up, our church had covered-dish dinners all the time. And my mamaw was the reigning fried chicken queen!"

"Ooh, and the ladies around here fix some of the best butter beans and fried catfish you'd ever want to eat." The pastor licked his lips, quickly realizing what he'd done. They both laughed.

"Sugar Mae Jacobson, that is the best-smelling sweet potato casserole I've ever caught a whiff of," Mamaw exclaimed.

"Mamaw! Mamaw!" Rosey said, tugging at Mamaw's dress.

"Rosey, Mamaw is talking, baby girl, and it isn't polite to interrupt. First graders should know that already."

"I know, Mamaw. I know. But Bobby Dean and Christopher told me that they had already divided all of your fried chicken up with the baseball team." Rosey paused to see if Mamaw understood the seriousness of the situation. "And, Mamaw," she said, trying to whisper now, "I just can't eat any more of Aunt Norma's chicken stuff. It don't—"

"It doesn't," Mamaw corrected.

"It doesn't even smell right."

Her mamaw's belly shook as she laughed. "Baby girl, you know your mamaw has you a piece of chicken tucked away. Your granddaddy's got some just for you and him and Charlotte. So you go over there and sit down by him, and he'll take care of you."

Dinner on the grounds of their little church was actually dinner in the parking lot. Because there weren't really any grounds. Just a lot of asphalt. But none of them cared. The ladies of this church had set up a feast. There were more casseroles and pies than you'd find in an entire year's subscription to *Southern Living*.

Rosey's mama and daddy sat down across from her after

she planted herself firmly under her granddaddy's arm. Charlotte sat beside her, whining about wanting a Coke and not sweet tea. Rosey didn't care what she drank as long as Granddaddy had her a chicken wing somewhere in his stash. That was Rosey's favorite piece of chicken. She liked it because her mama had always liked it.

Rosey watched as her mama patted her daddy's arm. She loved to watch them touch and kiss. Whatever it was they had, Rosey sure knew that she wanted some of it too. One day. But not right now. She still thought boys were gross! Especially if they were like her cousin Bobby Dean. Because he flat drove her crazy.

"Shoo!" her mamaw said as she sat down on the other side of Charlotte, swatting at flies.

"Why do you keep swatting at those flies, Mamaw? They ain't going nowhere. They just keep landing when you're not looking."

"You got to stay on them, Red," her granddaddy said. "Let those flies have the butter, and next thing you know, they'll want your biscuits too. You've got to be vigilant about some things in life. Ain't that right, Mama?"

"That's right," Rosey's mamaw said with another swat.

It wasn't until later that Rosey realized how true those words were. Because her failure to stay after the flies on the butter had allowed them access to the biscuits too.

"The women always drive themselves crazy swatting at flies, though." Rose said, returning to the small country church, noticing that the pastor was now gazing between the shutter slats out the front window.

"Those flies love them covered-dish dinners, don't they?"

"You're not joking," she replied.

She reached for the door handle. He turned around and placed his hand on hers. "Can I pray for you before you leave, Rose?"

His question startled her. "Um, I . . . well, I . . ." She thought her hesitation might afford him a change of mind. He simply stared at her. Waiting. She had rarely been known for her rudeness. Impatience maybe, but not rudeness. "I guess that would be okay."

Both of their hands still remained on the door handle. Hers for a quick exit. His as a preventative measure. He laid his other hand on her shoulder. They closed their eyes. "Our dear Father, You know, life has so many directions to take nowadays." He sighed heavily. "So many directions and ways to go, people just get lost along the way. I pray that You would let Rose here know that no matter how lost she may feel, she's never so lost that she can't find her way back home. Back home to You. Amen."

She couldn't even muster a smile when he finished.

They opened the door together, and a cold gust blasted them. She took off toward her car. "Then you have never been as lost as me, Pastor Johnson," she whispered to the wind. "You've never been as lost as me."

But Pastor Johnson heard her, because the wind carried her words straight to his heart. Tiny drops of freezing rain began to fall as he closed the door tightly. He shifted the shutter slats to catch sight of her as she drove away, then picked up his cell phone and made a call to his nephew, who lived with him and his wife at the parsonage while the young man studied at the seminary. Something tugged at him that Rose still needed a little help with her journey.

20

Rose listened to the pellets of frozen rain pop against her windshield, trying to shake off the preacher's words. Lost things were rarely found. If anybody knew that, she surely did. What had been lost between her and Jack couldn't be found. What she had lost by her affair couldn't be undone. What her mother had lost with her father would never be restored. Lost things don't get found, no matter how Pollyannaishly people wanted to live their lives. Rose was educated enough and wise enough to know that truth.

The ringing of her phone registered Charlotte's number. She welcomed the distraction. She pressed the phone icon on her steering wheel. "What's up?" she asked.

"Child, you better bring your Advil. Uncle Leonard and Aunt Lola just got here, and they brought all twelve of their grandchildren. Not a parent in sight to take care of them, but twelve spawn of someone else's are now here in this house. They better not think I'm watching them."

Rose couldn't help but laugh. "Send them to the backyard."

"It's subzero out there." Charlotte paused. "That is a wonderful idea! Come on, kids, put on your coats and get outside. Those floodlights are bright enough; you'll think it's afternoon!"

"You are shameless."

"It was your idea," she chided. "And should anybody ask, I'll let them know it too. Now, where are you?"

"Who knows? At this point I'm just driving, hoping I'll get there before tomorrow. But maybe if I wait long enough, you'll have all of those kids asleep before I get there."

"These kids are not—"

"Shhhhh."

"These kids are not"—Rose could hear that she spoke through clenched teeth—"spending the night here. There is a motel up the street, and I hope Uncle Leonard brought his credit card, because those children look like some hungry, wild beasts."

"I'll pick up the Advil."

"No. Liquor. Advil wouldn't break through all this pain."

Rose laughed again. "I have a question. How do you spell Shayrun?"

"Is this a trick question?" Charlotte popped her gum.

"No," she chuckled. "I'm serious. How do you spell Shayrun?"

"It's like everybody spells Shayrun. S-h-a-r-o-n."

Rose would officially go to her grave never forgiving herself for having spent a large portion of her life being an idiot. "Of course," she replied. "That's how I thought you spelled it."

"Well, honey, if you're having trouble with words like that, you might better get you a tutor before you embarrass yourself."

"You may be right," Rose assured her.

"Oh, honey, I have got to go. Aunt Lola just pulled out the biggest chocolate cake I've ever seen. Lord have mercy, there are more cakes around here. I'm telling you, if they put candles on these cakes, we'd go up in flames. You better get here quick while I still have all those children outside, away from the food . . . Well, here, your brother wants to talk to you again anyway."

"Hey," came Christopher's welcome voice. "I forgot to tell you this morning that I thought maybe we could have a Christmas dinner with Mom, since you're going to be home and it's so close to the holidays."

Well, his voice *had* been welcome. Rose felt her smile evaporate. Amazing how quickly that could happen. "Yeah, I guess you did forget to tell me that."

"You really need to spend some time with her, and I know you won't be back for Christmas, so let's at least do this." She could hear the intense desire in his voice.

"You know, I don't know why all you people make such a

big deal out of Christmas anyway. I can't remember a Christmas that was any good," she retorted.

"Then you have a very selective memory. And if you
would quit thinking about yourself long enough, you might
remember some good things about your life."

She refused to let him hear her hurt. He had no idea what
she had been remembering over the last several hours. But
there was nothing good about Christmas. Absolutely nothing
that she could remember. Then she remembered.

———

Rosey slammed the large Sears catalog onto the kitchen table.
Jenny climbed into the vinyl-covered seat next to her.

"What you got there, girls?" Mamaw asked.

"We're picking out what we want Santa to bring us," Rosey
confirmed as she opened the first page of what seemed to be a
gazillion-page catalog. Jenny started oohing and aahing as soon
as she opened it.

Rosey crinkled her brow and told her, "That's not even the
toys, Jenny!"

"Well, get on to the toys then!" Jenny bopped in her seat.

"You girls want some hot chocolate with marshmallows?"

Rosey and Jenny jerked their heads in tandem.

And for the next hour, Rosey, Jenny, and Mamaw sipped
hot chocolate and wrote out their wish lists to Santa Claus. By
the time they were finished, Mamaw had outdone them both.

"Does Santa come to old people?" Rosey asked her daddy when she got home that night and replayed their afternoon for him.

"Santa can come to older people, I'm sure," he said.

"Well, I've never seen you or Mama get nothing from Santa, so I didn't know if he'd want to bring Mamaw something or not. But I didn't want to tell her and hurt her heart, because she really, really, really liked this thingamajig that she said could wash her clothes real fast."

"Do you think it was a washing machine?" he prodded.

"Yeah, maybe it was one of those."

Rosey's daddy scooped her up in his arms and headed toward the staircase and then up to her room. "Well, Santa always knows what we like, so who knows? Maybe this year Mamaw will get something special for Christmas."

"I think she's been pretty nice. I mean, I'm not sure what a mamaw could do to be naughty and all, but she hasn't missed church since I've known her."

Her daddy chuckled, and she felt the warmth of his breath as he rested his head against her cheek. "Then I'm certain she'll get that thingamajig that washes her clothes real fast."

When Christmas Eve arrived, Rosey's family spent the night at Mamaw's house. They did every Christmas Eve. That's just how it was. And everyone knew that they were not allowed to see their gifts until Daddy brought out the big camera with the spotlight on top and made movies of the whole thing. But this year Rosey just had to investigate something for herself.

So sometime in the middle of the night, Rosey sneaked out of bed. She couldn't fall asleep anyway, so she tiptoed to the family room. That's where Santa came, because that's where the fireplace was. But Rosey was going because she only needed to know one thing. All she needed to know was that Santa had come for Mamaw, because if he hadn't, she would have to share her gifts, because Mamaw couldn't be disappointed on Christmas. That would just be more than Rosey could bear.

Rosey rounded the corner, the pine planks cold on her bare feet. She put her hands over her eyes, peering through the spaces between her fingers. She didn't want to spoil her own surprise, so with a smaller window to see things through, she wouldn't see as much. She began her visual scan at the left side of the fireplace. About halfway through her survey, she caught sight of it. Santa had come for Mamaw too! A big ol' washing thingamajig was in the middle of the family room floor, with something else just as big beside it. Well, that was all she needed to know.

Rosey crept over to Mamaw and Granddaddy's bedroom door, which had been left ajar. She peeked through the small crack. Mamaw was on her side of the bed, facing the door, and Rosey could see Granddaddy tucked behind her with his hand draped halfway around her. Her stomach was a little too expansive for his arm to span the entire distance, but it fit there perfectly, Rosey thought. She looked at Granddaddy's face lying above Mamaw's. They both looked a little funny to her without their glasses on. She figured their teeth were in the bathroom, in a cup. For a moment she wondered what else they took off before they went to bed.

But seeing them there made Rosey completely happy. And she knew this would be the best Christmas they had ever had. She knew it because Santa had come to see Mamaw too. In fact, the whole turn of events made Rosey so completely content that instead of waking everyone up in the dead of night to see their presents, she crawled into bed with Christopher and slept until the sun came up. In the morning everyone was surprised that she had slept so long, but they didn't know Rosey had already had Christmas.

———

"Rosey? Are you there?" Christopher asked.

"Yeah, I'm here," she replied, worrying a little that the ice seemed to be winning the battle with her windshield wipers. She turned on her defrost. "But I just don't like Christmas anymore, Christopher. I can't help it. It has too many old memories."

"I know. That's why it's time you start making new memories. I'm sure you and Jack have had *some* good Christmases together."

Rose had told Christopher most of what was going on with her and Jack, at least what she could bear to talk about. "I really don't want to talk about Jack either."

"Listen, Rosey, I know that one Christmas was horrible. I know you've never been hurt so deeply before or since, but I also know that you have got to get rid of all this. It's eating you alive."

Memories bombarded her now. The crying. The yelling. The Christmas tree and packages that were underneath it. Rose tried to stop the memories, but she couldn't. They were coming now, fast and strong and loud. What she had been refusing to think about for years was surging to the surface like a tsunami. And she was sure its arrival would destroy any life that remained.

———

Rosey heard the screaming from down the hall. She was only thirteen and could count on one hand the times that she'd heard her parents argue.

Her heart thumped hard and fast in her chest. She slid out of bed and tiptoed with bare feet through the carpeted doorway and into the hall. She peered around the corner and into the family room, where she saw the back of her mama's head and the side of her daddy's face as his anger seeped all the way down the hall and struck Rosey in the pit of her gut.

"I won't live this way anymore," Rosey's daddy yelled.

Her mama sobbed frantically. "But I'm sorry. I'm so sorry," she pleaded. "It was a mistake. I never should have let it happen. It didn't mean anything."

Rosey thought maybe her mama was apologizing for the country-style steak she'd forgotten the previous night in the Crockpot. The house was still filled with the scorched smell. She wasn't sure why a burned dinner would lead to yelling. But if it did, she was certain she would make sure she never burned dinner herself.

"You are not sorry. And this probably isn't the first time."

"I'll do anything," her mama screamed. "Anything. Please tell me what I can do."

Rosey heard a tremble in her father's next words. "There are no more anythings. You've used up all your anythings."

Her daddy got up and started down the hall. Rosey's bedroom was too far away for her to make it back there unde-tected. Instead, she slipped into her parents' bedroom, flung herself to the opposite side of the bed, and scooted under-neath it. The blue bed skirt rippled with the wind her quick movements brought. The minute she was hidden, her daddy came in, and she felt the bed move with the weight of what must have been a suitcase as it landed roughly on the end of the bed. Her mama rushed in and threw her body across the bed. "No! You can't! What about the children?"

She felt her mama's weight being shifted. "You should

have thought about the children." His voice had grown calm and steady. "But you never think about anyone but yourself. I hope those other men made you happy. Because that's what you have traded this family for."

Rosey's mind coursed through a thousand thoughts. What did he mean by "other men"? Rosey knew her mother had been gone a lot. She said it was all the real estate she was selling. That's what she had started doing after they moved to Myrtle Beach. Rosey had never liked it there. Everything had changed. Their lives. Their home. Even the way her mama and daddy looked at each other. If only her mama wasn't such a bad cook. If only she hadn't burned the dinner.

The repeated sound of hangers scraping the metal clothes rack passed through Rosey's bombardment of thoughts, and each time she heard the scraping, the weight of the luggage grew.

Rosey heard the zip and felt the weight lift. She listened as her daddy's shoes walked toward the door.

"I'm sorry! I'm so sorry!" her mother screamed. "And there weren't men. It was just one. And he didn't mean anything to me. You're the only one that has ever meant anything to me. Just you! No one means anything to me but you."

Rosey heard nothing but her father's fading footsteps amid her mother's wails.

"Daddy! Daddy!" Rosey cried as she crawled out from under the bed and ran to him. "Daddy, please don't go. I'll cook for you. I won't ever let your dinner burn again. Daddy, please don't go!" He put down the suitcase.

She clung to his waist. The strong arms of her gentle father wrapped around her. He lifted her face and kissed it. "Shh . . . baby girl," he whispered into her ear. "Shh . . . This has nothing to do with your dad's dinner. And I'm not leaving you. Okay? I just can't stay here with Mom anymore."

Rosey's head was spinning. She saw her mama wrapped in a ball on the edge of the bed, crying, gasping for air. She wanted to cut herself in half. Make herself a rubber band or something and wrap them all together so no one could leave. Anything to make this stop happening. She squeezed her daddy tighter. "You can't leave me, Daddy!" She used her fists to beat against his chest. "Take me with you, please, Daddy. Take me with you!"

She wrapped her arms tightly around his neck. But her daddy gently unfolded them and moved her body back as much as she would allow. He looked into her eyes. "You know you're my heart, don't you, baby girl?"

"Yes, Daddy."

"And I will always love your mama, and you are so much like her," he said, chuckling through tears that had begun to fall. "But you have to listen to your daddy."

"I don't want to listen if you say you're leaving," Rosey declared, slapping her hands against her ears.

He pulled them away and smiled the smile that always let

Rosey know things would be okay. But somewhere in her erratically beating heart, she knew that smile didn't have the same meaning this time. "Now, listen," he said, "Daddy is not leaving you, baby. I can see you every day. Just let me get settled, and we'll figure all this out. But we can't figure it all out today. So you just have to trust me, okay? I am not leaving my children. Daddy loves you and Christopher with all of his heart. Now, I have to go." He kissed the top of her head and took his suitcase and headed to the door.

Rosey followed, screaming. Crying and screaming. Her heart was officially breaking. As she reached for the screen door to follow her daddy onto the walkway, a hand grabbed her arm.

"You can't go, Rosey." She dimly heard Christopher's voice speak into her ear.

"I've got to go!" she wailed. "Daddy's leaving! We've got to make him stay!"

Christopher pulled her to him and wrapped his arms around her. She collapsed to the floor, sobbing, Christopher with her, protecting her. He always protected her. "You'll see Dad again," he said, kissing her hair.

Rosey wept fitfully there on the floor. And somewhere in her tears, strangers arrived. They were fear and anger. But she let them stay until eventually they became her faithful companions. And the peace that passes understanding had been relegated to foolish childhood memories.

21

The freezing rain intensified as Rose struggled to see the road clearly. Her breath was coming in pants, and her chest was hot. She tried to keep from shouting. It was useless. "I have no desire, Christopher, to have anything to do with celebrating Christmas with Mother!" The anger had to be released, even though Christopher wasn't the target. Because everything inside her felt as if it were on fire.

He tried to temper her outburst. "You need to calm down."

"Calm down?" she screamed. "I don't want to calm down! I hate that woman, do you understand that? That woman is why I don't want children! That woman is why I am the way I am! That woman is why my marriage is in shambles. And THAT WOMAN"—Rose's fury peaked—"IS WHY MY FATHER IS DEAD!"

"Now, hold on a minute, Rosey," Christopher said in a severe tone. "You act like she killed him with her own two hands."

"She might as well have! You know what the doctors said. They said that there was absolutely no cause for his death that they could find, but for some reason it was like his heart just collapsed! What do you call that? I say he died because she broke his heart! And that is why I'm not coming there for any other reason than . . . OH GOD!"

———~———

A dark shadow appeared in front of Rose. The death angel had come. "Can you move, ma'am?" the young voice asked.

She hadn't anticipated that the death angel would talk, but she was in too much pain to care. "It hurts," she said.

As her mind began to wash away with the icy rain, the death angel encouraged her to hold on. She heard the Jaws of Life tear at the metal wrapped around her. Then, strangely, she heard the death angel ask the ambulance driver if he could ride with her. That his uncle really wanted him to stay with her all the way.

The last thing Rose heard was the shutting of the ambulance door. And with it, she was certain, the ending of her life as well.

———~———

Dr. Dirk Palmer ran scores of tests and could find nothing more than a concussion. But his patient was still nonresponsive, so he made the decision to put her in intensive care, just so the nurses could keep a close watch on her during the night. The small cut above her eye required only four small stitches that would dissolve by themselves in about ten days. His patient never moved the entire time he sewed them.

Had Rose been awake, she would have refused to allow this man to touch her, because his name sounded way too much like that of a soap-opera doctor. She had refused treatment before for the same reason. Well, no, actually that one had reminded her of Rick Springfield when he played a doctor on *General Hospital*. Back when she and her mamaw would sneak and watch the show together. That was the real reason she wouldn't let that doctor touch her. He couldn't be a real doctor looking like Rick Springfield.

Dr. Palmer made sure she was settled into ICU before he took a break. His shift was scheduled to be over at ten that night, but when the time came and Rose still was not responsive, he decided to stay a little longer. He lived in Wilmington, almost an hour away. He had wanted to be a small-town doctor, but his wife's family had lived in Wilmington all their lives. So the compromise was his commute.

He went to the small office, sat down on the lumpy couch, and made a call. "Hey, baby. Did I wake you?"

He could hear the grogginess in his wife's voice. "I just laid my head down. The girls were exceptionally wired tonight," she said with a soft laugh.

"I think I'm going to spend the night here tonight. There's this patient"—he paused, not certain of his own feelings—"I just think I need to be here."

"You do what you need to do, honey. We'll be here in the morning, waiting for you."

He loved this woman, whom he could envision sleeping in his T-shirt, because she liked his smell. "I'll be home shortly."

He stretched out on the couch and closed his eyes. But he kept his soul wide-awake.

Rose was having a nightmare. Surely that's what all the darkness was. Until she saw a blinking light at the side of her head; then she thought maybe she was just dead. The sad part about being dead, however, was that this blinking red light was a far cry from all of the bright lights people who were dying had reported through the years. It didn't surprise her much. Nothing happened for her the way it did for other people. Plus, the way she'd been living, it was a wonder she saw any light at all.

Her eyes slowly adjusted to her surroundings. She noticed more blinking lights, sensed intruders up her nostrils, and felt a stinging pain in her right hand. She allowed her left hand to slowly peruse the vicinity. She felt the IV in the top of her other hand and gasped. Then her fingers drifted up to her nose and discovered the small plastic tubing. She wasn't dead; it was worse. She'd been snatched by aliens and become a cloning project.

Her eyes focused more, and two women materialized outside her door, wearing odd-looking matching outfits. Then she realized where she was. The incessant beeping noise made the revelation completely clear. She was in the hospital. She bolted upright in the bed and heard the crinkling sound of the pillow as it rushed back to its prehead shape.

She reached for buttons, any buttons, and she pushed all of them as crazily as she'd ever pushed anything before. This experience sure didn't feel anything like the one Christopher had described when she had gone to see him. No, she was certain she smelled death here.

She pushed herself out of the bed, causing alarms to sound off everywhere. The twins opened the glass door and rushed into her room just as her activity knocked over a cart that was somehow attached to her body.

"Ma'am, ma'am, you've got to relax! Please, sit down," urged the tall, skinny one, taking Rose by the arm. The short, heavy one stooped to pick up Rose's mess.

Rose jerked her arm away. "I will not sit down! And one of you little blue people had better explain to me what in the world all of these—these"—she motioned to the attached paraphernalia—"all of these tubes are doing sticking out of me."

She ripped the oxygen from her nostrils as the two nurses made ineffectual attempts to calm her.

The tubes' departure made her sneeze. And all the movement made her woozy. The two blue women barely caught her, then maneuvered her to sit safely on the edge of the bed.

A man in a white lab coat appeared at the door. "Well, well, I see our patient has risen."

Rose regained her composure. "Patient? I'm nobody's patient!" she exclaimed. "I'll have you know there is nothing wrong with me, and I don't know how in the world you got me here, but I will not be poked and prodded like a lab rat." She stood up again, spying the door. She decided to make a dash for it past the three onlookers, but suddenly felt a breeze tickle her southern region. She twisted her head around only to see a bare behind. Hers. She jerked the edges of the worn pink nightgown together and planted herself firmly back down on the bed. She touched her head, which was throbbing. "Oh my word, what happened to my head?"

The doctor rolled a stool over and sat down in front of her. He pulled a silver penlight from his top pocket and used two fingers to widen her eye. She flinched. "You had an accident. You've got a bad concussion and had to have a few stitches."

She rubbed her head again.

"But otherwise I'd say you're a miracle." He shined the light in her other eye. "By what they tell me of the status of your car, I'd say that your being alive, never mind pretty much normal"—he emphasized the "pretty"—"means you have much to be thankful for."

Rose stayed on the edge of the bed, digesting it all. Slowly the wreck came back. The lights, the swerving, the ice, the crash. She had been on the phone. Yes, she had been on the phone with Christopher. Talking about . . . talking about . . . oh, that's right, they were talking about *her.*

"Well, if there's nothing wrong with me, then I'd appreciate your letting me go home."

Dr. Palmer replaced his penlight, stood up, and pushed his stool back. "Well, I'm sorry, Ms. Fletcher, but you won't be going home tonight. I can put you in a regular room, though. And we can take some of this 'stuff' off of you." He smiled. "I'll get you something for the pain."

He picked up her chart and wrote on it, then handed it to the tall, scrawny nurse. "I see, Dr. Palmer. I'll call the third floor," she said as she headed out the still-open door.

"Dr. Palmer, huh?" Rose questioned, aborting a new attempt to stand up as her head swam. "What's your first name?"

"Doctor," he replied, a tiny quirk at the corner of his lips. He was gone before she could reply.

The nurses moved her to a new room and offered her two little blue pain pills. Rose protested until the pain pulsed. She was snoring in minutes.

22

Rose woke up in her new room sometime in the wee hours of the morning, with a splitting headache and a screaming stomach. The entire hospital experience had to register again before she realized exactly where she was. But the sterile smell brought it all back quickly. She swung her feet over the side of the bed but decided she'd take the getting out of it a little more slowly this time. She hadn't forgotten what sudden movement had done to her previously.

The cold floor sent a shock wave through her system. "These people should supply footies," she told the darkness. Then she felt the draft on her backside again and pulled her gown together. "And some robes," she huffed.

She walked over to the closet, the door of which was

standing ajar, and peeked inside. Her purse was on the shelf, and her suitcase was on the floor. She sighed with relief.

Scratches covered the purse, but there wasn't major damage, and her wallet was still inside. She pulled it out but then remembered that she didn't have any cash. That was why she'd had to use her credit card at Fletcher's Drugstore. The memories of the day were coming back piece by piece. She opened the wallet anyway. And tucked neatly inside, behind her checkbook holder, she found three crisp, folded one-dollar bills. She couldn't believe it. She had searched that exact compartment earlier, she was certain.

Her stomach spoke again. She didn't waste time trying to figure out how the money had gotten there; she had more immediate needs to focus on. She cracked her door open and peeked into the well-lighted hall. She wasn't sure why she felt that she needed to sneak, but something about hospitals gave her the feeling she should probably let someone know when she was getting out of the bed. Of course, she didn't do too well with rules of any kind, so getting permission for a food excursion wasn't on her agenda.

She crept quietly up the hall and was followed only by the buzz of the fluorescent lights that established her way. She heard a few voices from around a corner and peeked to see who was there. Two different ladies in blue were in the middle of the hall behind a desk, drinking from paper cups with straws and chatting away.

Oh my word, Rose thought suddenly. *Where is my phone? Nobody knows where in the world I am. I was talking to Christopher. He probably thinks I'm dead or something. I've got to find a phone!* Her stomach growled. *Well, I've got to eat first, and then I'll call him.*

She crossed the hall in front of the nurses when their backs were to her. She took the stairs down a couple of floors, figuring the cafeteria was on a lower level. She opened the door gently at floor two and sneaked out into another hallway. A sign declaring "Cafeteria/Vending Machines" was like a bright light at the end of her tunnel. She hadn't died, so at least she should be rewarded with food.

She hurried toward the suppliers of food and beverage and stopped before them with great joy and satisfaction. She was even more grateful to find they took dollar bills. She started with the beverage machine first. The sound of the bottle falling through the machine almost made her cry. She had officially had more Cokes in a twenty-four-hour period than she had had for the last fifteen years.

She deposited the dollar into the food machine. She didn't even know what to get out of there. She hadn't eaten chips in forever. She saw a bag of sour cream and onion ones and figured she had no one to impress, so she might as well go all out.

She stuck her dollar in and pushed A6, and the black spiral holder began to swirl. She monitored the chips as they began to fall. But they stopped halfway and successfully lodged between the Toastchee crackers and the Snickers bars.

"You have got to be kidding me," Rose said, punching the Plexiglas. It didn't budge. She put her hands on both sides and shook as best she could, hoping she would dislodge the food and not something in her pounding head.

"That won't do it," a frail yet clear voice called from behind her.

Rose turned around to see a small elderly woman standing with a walker, wearing a gown that peeked out from underneath her silky pale pink robe. She was grinning at Rose with her head cocked and the back of her hair pushed toward the front as if she'd been lying on it for a long time.

"You have got to give it a little hip action," she said as she scooted her way around to the side of the machine. She moved away from the walker and gave the machine a little hit with her tiny hip. Rose thought the lady might break her entire left side with that whack, as frail as she looked.

But the potato chips dislodged immediately. Rose perked up. Obviously she had done this before. "You're good."

"I'll be even better if you've got enough money to get me some of those regular M&M's," she said with a glint in her eyes, raising her eyebrows up and down.

Rose eyed her last dollar as if it were gold. She scrunched her lips like Elvis and hoped the lady didn't want a drink too. Rose let her dollar slide into the machine.

"It's C5," offered the little voice.

Obviously the little lady got these often too. Rose punched

C5 and the M&M's fell without incident. Rose pulled them from the vending machine and handed them to her. "There you go."

"Why, thank you, Red. Now, come on, follow me." She started scooting away.

Rose stared at her. The only one who called her Red was her granddaddy. "Well, I would love to, but actually, I really have to get back to my room and call my brother," Rose protested.

The little lady turned around and used her index finger to give a come-hither motion. "He'll find you, Red. Don't you worry. He'll find you. So come on with me."

Rose eyed the odd, scooting figure and wondered how in the world she knew that Christopher would find her. Obviously she was just speculating that whoever was searching for her would eventually find her. But she had piqued Rose's interest. After all, why should the whacked events of her day stop here, in the corridor of a hospital, staring at processed food, before following a strange old lady to who knows where? After all, twenty-four hours had not officially passed, so it was still the same crazy day that she had started.

Rose followed the white-headed, pressed-haired, half-scalp-revealed, walker-scooting vending-machine companion up the hall, around the corner, and through some swinging double doors before they came to a halt in front of another door. The tiny figure opened it and flipped on a light switch as she entered. A low light filtered through the room. She backed up to the edge of the bed and sat down.

"You wouldn't mind helping me get all the way in, would you?" she asked Rose. "I'm still a little weak."

"Uh, sure. Yeah, I guess I can." Rose set her Coke and chips down on the small table next to the bed. She moved the walker to the foot of the bed and gave the light body a lift until the lady was firmly in the middle of the bed. Rose picked her feet up and helped her turn them; then the lady scooted herself back comfortably. Rose fluffed her pillows and watched as she leaned back into them with a loud sigh.

The stranger reached over to the bedside tray on the opposite side and picked up a cup. "Do you mind giving me a swig of your soda?" she asked, extending the cup in Rose's direction.

Rose was absolutely certain she had never met a more aggressive person in her life. The entire world thinks that Northerners are pushy, but she was certain it was the other way around. And the simple fact that Southerners did it with accents reminiscent of Scarlett O'Hara made it somehow less offensive.

The stranger patted the side of the bed with a delicate, wrinkled hand. "Here, take a load off, and give me a little sip."

Rose tried not to look amazed. "I'll give you a little sip, ma'am, but I really can't stay," Rose said, unscrewing the lid of her Coke.

The lady patted the bed again. "You don't have a place to

go until your brother gets here, Red, so why don't you just sit down and spend some time with a little old lady who has been having some trouble sleeping. We'll eat, chat, and then both get a better night's sleep."

Rose knew she looked bewildered now. There was simply no way to hide it. But much to her own dismay, she sat on the edge of the bed and poured the little lady some of her Coke.

The woman sat forward and took a long drink. Rose studied the lines around her lips as they pressed around the cup. She had to be eighty if she was a day. "Ahhhh," she said, leaning back into her pillow and closing her eyes. "There will be Coca-Cola in heaven. I'm just certain of it."

Rose held her bottle in one hand but still hadn't opened her bag of chips. All she could do was stare at the little lady.

Suddenly the lady jerked forward and opened her eyes. Rose jerked backward. The lady's eyes twinkled with mischief. The green of them was strikingly brilliant and clear. "You want to share your chips, and I'll share my M&M's?"

Rose didn't know why this lady thought Rose wanted her snacks to become the midnight buffet, but the childlike smile was irresistible. "Sure, you can have some of my chips," she said, setting the Coke between her legs so she could open the bag. She started to extend her chips, then pulled them back close, smiling. "But you have to share your M&M's too." Rose set the bag on the bed.

"I'll share my M&M's and some of my other stash with

you. I've got all kinds of goodies," the little old lady said, reaching crooked fingers over to the drawer in her bedside tray. She opened it with excitement, revealing a stash of candy the likes of which Rose hadn't seen since her cousin Bobby Dean had robbed the 7-Eleven. She had Skittles and chewing gum and candy bars. "I've got plenty to share," she assured Rose, then reached into the potato chip bag.

Rose picked up her Coke and took a long drink. She could never tell anyone she'd been drinking these. Anyone who knew her would be convinced she had officially fallen off the deep end. She settled it back between her legs and reached for a chip. "Well, since we're sharing our midnight snack, don't you think we should know each other's name?"

The little lady pulled a tissue from behind her pillow and wiped her fingers on it, then extended her hand. "Well, excuse me for my rudeness. My name is Abigail Turner, and I would be privileged to know your name."

"My name is Rose," she said, shaking Abigail's hand.

Abigail's eyes grew extremely large. "Rose?"

"Yes, ma'am, Rose."

"Huh, well, um . . ." She gazed downward and fidgeted with the bag of M&M's. "Rose is a very pretty name. Is that your only name?" she asked, finally returning her eyes to her bed companion.

Rose laughed. "No, I have more. It's Rose Fletcher."

"Hmm, Rose Fletcher. Well, it's very nice to meet you

denise hildreth

Rose, Rose Fletcher." She dug in the bag for another chip and
then leaned back once more on her pillow. She offered Rose
an M&M from her other hand, which she accepted. "What's
that bandage on your head for?"

Rose reached up to touch it. The pain had eased.

"Why do people always do that?"

Rose's expression turned puzzled. "Do what?"

"Touch things someone asks them about before giving an
answer, as though they're not quite sure the other person
really saw what they saw."

Rose could tell Abigail's mind wasn't deteriorating at the
rate of her body. "You know, I've never thought about that
before." She chuckled. "Maybe we could find out someday."

"We'd make millions!" Abigail exclaimed, tossing her free
hand in the air. "And then if we could figure out why every
time someone eats something that tastes horrible, they stick it
in someone else's face and say, 'Here, you try this,' we'd make
millions again!"

She sure was an excitable little creature. "I'd say we'd
make tons on that one too." Rose laughed.

Abigail's expression changed immediately. "So tell me
again about that Band-Aid."

"Well, I had a car accident last night."

"Oh, Red, are you all right?" she asked, leaning back up
off her pillow.

"I think so. Nothing much more than a few stitches. I

mean, it's apparent nothing has happened to my appetite," she said, lifting her Coke and taking another swallow.

"You want to taste something really good?" Abigail's expression grew as mischievous as Charlotte's used to be.

"You have something better than we're already eating?"

She nodded in affirmation. Then she reached behind her back pillow and pulled out a jar of peanut butter. Her smile grew wider and wider the farther that jar got into the room.

Rose wasn't sure what else she might try to pull from behind that pillow of hers.

Then, from the drawer, Abigail pulled two plastic packages of utensils and napkins. "I saved the silverware from the lunch my daughter brought me. And she sneaked in the peanut butter for me. You've got to try this," she said, poking a package in Rose's direction. They tore them open to get the spoons.

Abigail took her spoon and dipped it into the jar. Then she dropped a couple of her M&M's on top of the scoop of peanut butter and began to eat from her spoon with obvious pleasure.

It sure looked good to Rose. Abigail thrust the jar in Rose's direction. Rose took a big, deep dip herself. They ate in silence for awhile. Too hard to talk with peanut butter in their mouths. Later, Rose attempted to speak through the stickiness. "Why are you here, Abigail?"

Abigail cocked her head. Rose had the urge to smooth the spikes of hair still sticking up. "They say I have cancer again.

Brought me here Monday, telling me I didn't have much more than a week left."

The bite Rose had just put in her mouth seemed to grow three sizes. She stared at the precious lady in front of her and wondered how God could allow such terrible things to happen to her. Then again, He'd let them happen to Rose.

Abigail must've seen the change in Rose's expression, because she leaned in close and whispered, "But you know, I just keep feeling better and better every day."

Rose tried to defuse the situation. "I'm so sorry, Abigail, you'd just never know."

"I know. That's what I keep trying to tell them." She gave a dainty cough, covering her mouth with another tissue.

Rose didn't know what else to say. The feelings of fear and doubt and all of her demons returned with those words that brought just one more curse of death. As if everything in life wasn't dead in her already. The people she loved. The parts of her heart that she used to treasure and guard. Her marriage.

"You don't have to get quiet, Red. If I'm not worried about it, you shouldn't worry your pretty head about it."

Rose couldn't help it; she had mastered the art of worrying. Why would she want to abandon something she had actually mastered? "How long have you had the . . . the . . . cancer?"

"Oh, you can say it, Red. It's called *cancer*. The big C. The curse of all curses. I had it awhile back. Then it went into remission, and now they say it has come back with a vengeance. But I'll be honest with you, I don't feel like there is a speck of it in this old body of mine." She licked her latest whopping spoonful of peanut butter, oblivious to the fact that she could actually be dying right there before Rose's eyes.

Rose studied her. "Well, you sure look good."

Abigail nodded her head adamantly. "I think so too. For a dying woman, anyway." She snickered.

"How is your daughter handling everything?" Rose asked, not feeling so hungry now.

"Oh, I have two girls, actually, and they are just little troupers." Her "girls" were probably in their fifties or sixties. Rose realized that to this lady, they would always be her little girls. "They sneak me in home cooking every night. And stay here around the clock. I made them go home tonight. I told them I would keep them awake all night long singing if they didn't leave. And, Red, if you heard me sing, you'd know that would terrorize anybody."

Rose watched her new friend. She wanted to enfold her tiny body into her arms and keep death at bay. But she just didn't want to deal with any more heartache tonight. And she really needed to call Christopher. He would be beside himself with panic.

Rose slid off the bed, her smile now faded to pity and pain. "Well, it was a pleasure sharing my vending snacks with you, Abigail."

"And it was a pleasure enjoying them." The little lady grinned. Rose wasn't sure whether they were her real teeth, but they looked good on her all the same.

Rose turned and headed for the door. As she gripped the door handle, Abigail remarked to the softly lit room, "Sleep well, my sweet Rose. And remember, His mercies are new every morning. You've just got to stop running *from* and start running *to*."

Rose's hand froze. And something entered the room that she hadn't felt since she was a little girl and the Spirit had fallen inside that country church on Dixon Street, and for a moment every demon in hell had to stand back from the war they had been waging for Rose.

23

Rose couldn't move. She couldn't turn around, and she couldn't leave. So she just stood there, gripping the handle as if it were her last great lifeline.

"There was a man once, Rose," Abigail continued softly. "A man who was crushed and hurt by the people he loved. In fact, his own brothers sold him and then went and told his dad he'd been killed. But if that wasn't enough, things got worse. He was thrown into prison for something he didn't do. Left in that prison, forgotten and alone. But there was something in him, Rose, that never allowed him to think that he was truly forgotten or truly alone. He always knew that somehow, some way, all the tragedy in his life, all the things that had been done wrong to him, the God of this universe, and the Creator of his very soul, would somehow make right."

Tears fell from Rose's eyes. Just as they had done most of the day. And she was unable to do anything to stop them.

"But one day, Rose, one day, the most powerful man in the nation heard about the man and brought him into his own world and made him the next man in charge. And do you know who eventually came to this former prisoner in their moment of need?"

Rose figured this was a rhetorical question, and sure enough, Abigail didn't wait for her to respond.

"The very brothers who had sold him. And do you know what he did?"

Rose's tears were dripping on her nightgown.

"He forgave them. That's what he did, Rose; he forgave them. And then, Rose, when he had children . . ." Abigail paused.

Rose gasped.

"He named them Manasseh and Ephraim. I know, odd names for your boys. But do you know what those names mean, Rose? Manasseh means 'the Lord has made me to forget.' And Ephraim means 'fruitful in the land of my affliction.'"

Rose squinted her eyes shut, trying to stop the deluge.

"I sure know that life brings tough roads. You know it too, I can tell. I've met people in these halls who are sick with all kinds of stuff, and some have as much money as God, and some don't have a nickel to their names. I've learned that storms don't care who you are, Rose. But I've learned something else—that the greatest fragrance comes out of a rose only when it has been crushed."

Everything in Rose wanted to run, but her body still wouldn't obey.

"You know the amazing thing about this man, Rose, is that his crushing made him great. But his forgiveness made him greater. And when he finally had those babies, Rose, he had forgotten the past and was finally able to see that his darkest torment had all been for the divine purpose. That tough places really can create amazing things."

Finally, Rose's hand obeyed. With every last bit of control she possessed, she quietly opened the door, walked through, and shut it. And then she ran. She ran as hard as she could run, back to the room she had come from, not caring anymore about the slit in her nightgown. And after a few wrong turns and a few wrong rooms, very much like her life, she finally found hers and threw herself across the bed. She cried until she fell asleep. Never remembering missed e-mails or phone calls or responsibilities. But sleep offered her no different words than the ones she had just heard.

———

A soft hand on her shoulder startled her. She bolted upright to see only the silhouette of a man whose face was unrecognizable because of the sun streaming so brilliantly through the open blinds of the window. For a moment Rose was certain she had finally made it to the bright light, and God had resorted to tapping people on the shoulders. Not such a different approach than the death angel's. Then God spoke.

"I've looked all over for you."

Well, that wasn't exactly what she thought God's first words to her would be, but she could certainly stay around to see where he was going next.

"Rosey." Hands took her by the shoulders.

She decided not to correct him. Plus, God had a strong grip.

Then he threw his arms around her. "I was so worried when the phone went dead."

"Christopher?" she whispered.

"Who did you think it was?" he asked in her ear.

"Well, after the last twenty-four hours I've had, I couldn't be certain."

He leaned back and looked at her. She looked back at his familiar and loving face. The face of the one who always showed up to rescue her. She grabbed him and hugged him as tightly as she had ever hugged him before. Then she suddenly remembered her dining companion from the evening before.

"Oh!" She pushed him back. "Sorry, but I've got to go see someone." She grabbed the folds of her gown and took off like a streak, minus the streaking, and headed to the second floor.

She heard Christopher following, but she couldn't stop to explain.

Rose burst into Abigail's room. No one was there but a strikingly large black orderly who was emptying the trash can. Abigail's bed was neatly made. Every sheet and blanket folded perfectly. All remnants of cups and M&M's and chips were gone. The tray that had been by the bed had been moved to the corner of the room. Rose jerked open its drawer. It was empty.

"Where is she?" Rose asked, terrified to hear the answer.

"Well, she's gone home, ma'am. She's finally gone home."

Anger filled her. "I knew it!" she screamed at the orderly. "See, it's morning! That's what He always does! He says His mercies are new every morning, and all He does is let people die and leave us here to pick up the pieces!"

The tall man looked at her calmly. She felt something inside of her begin to tremble. And the same feeling that had permeated her last night as Abigail spoke returned, magnified. "I think you might've misunderstood me, ma'am." His words were firm. "Miss Abigail went to her home, home. Up the street here in Whiteville. Seems like all that cancer couldn't be found on any of those tests she took yesterday. Not a trace. Can you believe that?" He shook his head slowly as he walked toward the door, where Christopher stood observing. "Not a trace."

Rose's mouth came agape.

As the orderly brushed past Christopher, he spoke again,

remembering. "I sure hope she got that flower she was waiting for."

"What did you say about a flower?" Rose inquired.

He turned around in the doorway. "Oh, she just said that
she was certain she didn't have any cancer but that she couldn't
leave until she got a rose she was waiting on. Said she had a
dream that she was going to get a very important rose and that
she couldn't leave until it got here. I'm guessing it must have
come yesterday."

And with that, he disappeared down the hall.

Rose felt the entire weight of the last twenty-four hours force
her to her knees. Christopher came to her side, knelt beside
her on the cold tile floor. She should've known this moment
had to happen. Because Christopher had told her years before,
"Eventually everyone has to break, or they'll simply live their
lives broken."

"I've been so wrong, Christopher." She stared out the
window at the gray sky. "Everything, my hatred, my marriage, my lies . . . Oh, God, how could I have been so stupid?"
She laid her head in her hands. Christopher took her in his
arms, just the way he did when Christmas boxes littered the
hallway.

"I wanted to make it all her fault. I wanted to make everything her fault, and then I became just like her. And I've hated

myself! I've hated myself so much!" Her words exploded through her hands.

"I know, Rosey, I know." Christopher stroked her hair.

"But I've been so wrong. And oh, God, all that I've done to Jack!" She raised her head, horrified by her actions. "All he did was love me. And I crushed him, Christopher. I crushed everything inside of him. And I did it mercilessly. I've hurt so many people. I've destroyed families! Here I am, the self-proclaimed advocate for children, who forgot to fight for her own. I am such a hypocrite, Christopher. I should have died in that wreck!" She pounded her chest.

"You *are* dying, Rosey." Christopher pulled her tighter and whispered into her ear. "You are dying. And you'll never be the same."

"But I just want to go back, Christopher! I just want to go back home. Before I hurt anybody. Before anybody hurt me. To the way it used to be. When we were little, and Mamaw and Granddaddy were there, and Mama and Daddy loved each other."

Christopher's tears began to fall at her words. "I know, Rosey. We all want to go back there. But we can't, baby girl. We can't go back. We can dream about it. Remember it. Talk about it. But we can't go back, Rosey. We can only go forward. And that's what you have to do. You have to go forward."

"But no one will be able to forgive the things I've done," she said, laying her head in the curve of his arm.

"People may not forgive, Rosey. But the One who truly forgives can and will. Don't you remember all those years ago when you made Mamaw have mercy on me? You stepped in for my fault. You were my mediator. My advocate. That's what has been done for you, Rosey. Your fault has been stepped into by the only one capable of redeeming."

And there on the floor of Abigail's hospital room, Rose found the forgiveness she had so desperately longed for. The demons were quieted once and for all. And the Rose who had always desired to live, the one who wasn't afraid—afraid to love, afraid to forgive, afraid to live—was the Rose who finally got up from the floor.

———

Christopher supported her as they walked back to her hospital room. When they got there, Dr. Palmer was standing at the foot of her bed, looking over her chart.

"Well, there you are, my little hospital traveler. How did you rest last night?"

She gave him a bleary-eyed look.

"I see." He smiled apologetically. "Well, the last round of your tests came back normal, and I'm discharging you. You're welcome to get dressed and have your brother here take you home. I trust you found your things in the closet?"

Rose nodded. The word *home* held new meaning this time. "Thanks."

He closed her chart, gave her a smile, and started for the door.

"But for the record"—she said, causing Dr. Palmer to stop—"you really do need to provide robes around here." Rose looked meaningfully at her hand, which was still holding closed the gap in her gown.

Dr. Palmer and Christopher laughed. "I'll see what I can do about that," Dr. Palmer said.

"Oh, and there is one thing. You never answered my question. What did you say your first name is?"

"I told you already. It's Doctor." He closed her door with a grin.

24

Rose asked Christopher to wait as she went into the restroom to change. She found her chocolate suit still neat and crisp beneath the tissue paper that she had wrapped it in for today's occasion. She donned a baby blue silk camisole to wear with it, and a pair of brown boots.

When she was finished dressing, Rose added a dainty brown beaded necklace and her diamond earrings. She tried to use her makeup to hide the dark circles from her long evening, then pulled her red hair back into a sleek ponytail. She replaced the bandage on her forehead with a tiny Band-Aid to hide the stitches. She studied herself in the mirror. Still tired looking, but the face that returned her gaze was finally one she recognized. A woman she had missed being and seeing.

Christopher helped Rose collect her things, and they headed for his car. She still felt woozy, so she didn't mind too much when a two-hundred-and-fifty-pound nurse named— yes, it was true—Bertha made it clear that Rose *would* ride in the wheelchair to the curb, whether she liked it or not.

Christopher made a quick call to Charlotte while Bertha situated Rose in the car. "You made all of them pray?" she heard him ask with a laugh. "All twelve of Uncle Leonard's grandchildren?"

Rose smiled. She figured her wreck had accomplished at least a couple of good purposes. It had gotten both herself and Charlotte praying.

"Have you heard any word on my car?" she asked as the sound of clicking seat belts filled the interior of Christopher's new Volvo. He and his wife had purchased it when they found out they were expecting their first child in the spring.

"Despite the fact that it helped save your life? Yeah, I hear you're going to need a new one."

"I had a feeling that would be the case. But at least I have clean underwear," she said, laying her head back slowly, try-ing to keep the trees outside from spinning. "Wonder where my phone ended up?" She chuckled.

"By the sound of the wreck, I would say it probably didn't fare much better than your car."

"Do you know how many e-mails I've probably missed?" she said, laughing harder. "I've probably got senators screaming because they haven't heard from me." Her laughter was clearly contagious, as Christopher started as well. "And Helen . . ." She couldn't stop now. "Whew . . ." She tried to regain her composure. It was useless. "Helen's probably downed a quart of vodka and a bottle of Valium."

That did it for both of them. "Hey," sputtered Rose, holding her side. "Watch where you're going."

"Yeah." He pulled himself together. "Don't need another wreck."

"Ow," she said, touching her head. "Who knew laughing could hurt your head?"

That made them start all over again. By the time they finally got control of themselves, they were turning onto Main Street in the small city of Mullins. They drove past at least three flower shops, the B. C. Moore's that had been there for at least a hundred years, Anderson Brothers Bank, and Aunt Norma's Alteration Shop. She smiled.

"Are you ready for what's ahead, Rosey?" Christopher asked, subduing any lingering humor.

"Are you talking about seeing Mother, or seeing Mamaw?"

"Both, I guess."

"Yes and yes. I think I've come to terms with everything that's happened."

Christopher turned toward Rose. "Do you want to call Jack?"

She sighed, trying to process all her thoughts. "No, not yet.

I have no idea what I would say. I might better take one thing at a time." She pulled down the visor and opened the mirror to check her bandage. "But would you mind if we just went somewhere first and got something to eat? I'm starving."

"Are you sure? There's enough food at Mamaw's to wipe out a quarter of world hunger."

She was certain that was true. "I just need a little while of just us. Me and you." She still enjoyed being his shadow.

"I'd like that. How about we go to Webster's Manor and get the country-cooking buffet. Oh, I'm sorry. That's right. You don't eat meat anymore, do you?"

That caused Rose to double over again. Except this time she could tell Christopher laughed only because she was laughing. When she regrouped, he asked, "Is that a yes or a no?"

Rose's stomach was beginning to remind her that she hadn't eaten since the huge meal Daisy had forced upon her. Except for the midnight snack, of course. She smiled at thoughts of Abigail dancing around her family room, popping M&M's into her mouth. "That's a 'why not?'"

Christopher pulled the car into the parking lot of Webster's Manor. The old Southern home on East James Street had been turned into a bed-and-breakfast years ago. They walked onto its large front porch and inside, across the hardwood floors. It was the beginning of the lunch crowd, and people in the South "did" lunch. Big lunches.

After they got situated in a booth, Rose ordered a Coke.

"You don't drink Coke," Christopher said as a declaration of truth, in case Rose had forgotten.

"I do now. Again," she said with a wink.

When their drinks came, Rose took a long, hard swig. "Do you ever stop and think about all of the crazy things we used to do when we were little? Remember when you got me to chase Beth Beatty out of the yard with boxing gloves on?"

"I was tired of her tormenting you on the bus every day," he said, drinking his sweet tea.

"Did it never cross your mind that my punishment would far outweigh my momentary satisfaction?"

"What, Mom making you kiss and make up bothered you?" He laughed.

Rose nodded and smiled. "That left me scarred." She studied their surroundings. She enjoyed the Southern accents and the laughter around her.

"Ever just wish you could do it all again?"

His dark eyes looked at her with the wonderment he had when they were growing up. "Sometimes. Sometimes I think about playing baseball until Mamaw hollered for us to come in for dinner."

They got up to fill their plates.

"You remember the time we were playing catch, and I told you to throw the ball harder, and it creamed me right in the nose? I bled for a good hour," she accused.

He smirked at her. "It was ten minutes at the most."

"Oh no, it was days . . ." She plopped a heaping pile of mashed potatoes on her plate and covered it with gravy.

Christopher poured vinegar over his collard greens. "Do you remember when me and Tom Patterson shot the BB gun at the car? And the driver saw us when we did it, and he turned the car around and found us and told our parents?"

"I remember you were scared." She paused. "You were scared to death."

"Yes, I was." He nodded.

She spooned out some sweet potato casserole. It was a starch kind of day. "Do you remember that morbid song that Granddaddy used to sing to us about the little girl named Marion Parker who got killed?"

He laughed one of those laughs of horror. "Who would make a song up about a dead child? It was so morbid."

"It was just wrong."

And over lunch they remembered. They remembered the place they had come from. They remembered the skinned knees and dime-store candy. They remembered the dreams of becoming Superman and Wonder Woman, or the next Donny and Marie, whichever found them first. They remembered the office they created in the attic and the fun they had in the world of make-believe and no responsibilities. And they just remembered everything that ever made them happy. Because Rose had realized home was now relegated to memories alone.

And when they were through remembering, they talked about where they were. Rose told of her last encounter with Jack, and Christopher described his baby's nursery in amazing detail, for a man.

After eating her last bit of banana pudding, Rose sighed. Christopher placed the receipt in his pocket. Rose reached to pull her wrap around her shoulders. But it wasn't there. Panic swept over her.

She jumped in her seat. "My shawl! Christopher, my cashmere wrap! I was wearing it during the wreck. Where is it? I've got to get it! It has to be okay. Hurry, we've got to check the car! I don't think it was in the suitcase." Tears were about to explode from her eyes.

They ran outside. He had the trunk open with a push of the button before they even reached the car. Rose jerked the suitcase open violently. She rummaged desperately but didn't see the chocolate color anywhere. Frantically she shoved the suitcase back to make room to check the side pockets. Nothing.

"Rosey. Rosey!" Christopher handed her what looked like a white kitchen garbage bag.

She yanked it toward her and tore it open. Folded inside were the clothes and shoes she had on during the wreck, including her beautiful cashmere wrap. She pulled it to her face and breathed in deeply. It still had that familiar smell that she loved. The smell of home. She felt herself lose control once again. But she knew she needed this cry too.

Christopher was still clueless about her emotion, but her patient brother just waited. Anyone who knew her well would understand that there were years of tears that still needed to come out of Rose.

"I'm sorry, Christopher. It's just . . ."

"You don't have to explain. Come on, let's go."

Rose freshened her makeup in the car and then reclined her chair, exhausted. The rest of the trip to see Mamaw held little conversation. Instead, she just watched the streets of Mullins pass by and calmed her spirit as best she could.

The Cox-Collins Funeral Home sign came into view. Cars had already begun to fill up the parking lot for the three o'clock service. Christopher pulled his car into a spot beside a black Ford Expedition. Rose didn't notice the SUV, because she was looking at the door of the funeral home where her precious granddaddy was waiting, staring in her direction.

She stepped out of the car, and her eyes filled with tears as she saw her granddaddy slowly lift his hand and the corner of his mouth turn up. As she shut the door and started up the sidewalk, a man in a black suit stepped out in front of her. She looked into his face. It was Jack. Her Jack. She tried to breathe.

"Jack, I—"

Jack placed his fingers over Rose's lips. "Not now. Right now, let's go see your granddaddy. He's waiting on you." He lightly touched her small Band-Aid, concern evident in his eyes. Then he brought his hand down and placed it gently around her own. It felt strangely perfect.

"But I've got to know, Jack. I've got to know. What kind of music do you like?"

"Rosey," he laughed softly. "Baby, that's not important right now."

She clutched his hand. "But it is, Jack. It's so important. I can't go in there unless I know."

"Okay, baby, calm down. I like old soft rock."

"Soft rock, huh?" She smiled.

"Yeah, that's what I like."

Then she nodded. And slowly they began to walk, Rose holding the hand of the man she loved. Followed by the man whom she had always loved. Walking toward the man who had always loved her. And surrounded by, for the first time, what she had so desperately longed for. Not *being* loved. No, Rose had always been loved. But *knowing* she was loved. She realized the big difference between the two. And for the first time since fear had invaded her life, it was now banished. Because for the first time in twenty years, Rose knew she was ready to love in return.

Rose linked her free arm through her granddaddy's as she reached his side.

"How's my Red?"

"Alive, Granddaddy. Finally alive." She tilted her head against his shoulder.

"I can see that, baby girl."

"I know what kind of music Jack likes, Granddaddy," she whispered to him.

He smiled his soft smile. "Ooh, that's good, baby girl. Your mamaw wanted that."

He patted her hand, then noticed her Band-Aid. "What happened to my Red?"

She returned the pat. She knew no one had told him of her accident. He didn't need anything else to trouble him. "Just a boo-boo, Granddaddy. Nothing but a boo-boo."

He leaned over and kissed her softly on her head, as he always had. "Well, look at that beautiful shawl. You kept your mamaw's shawl all these years?"

"Wrapped it right around my heart."

She and Jack walked in cadence with his slow shuffle up the stairs. "Are you ready to see Mamaw?"

Rose stopped when they reached the black-painted wooden door. She looked into her granddaddy's eyes. Jack squeezed her hand. She breathed in and felt the air flow freely. "Yes, Grandaddy, I'm ready to see Mamaw."

And in Rose went to see Mamaw, for the last time.

acknowledgments

I've always been amazed at the mind's ability to remember. There are even moments when you remember details that had been lost until the memory restored them. I've also been amazed at the power of a song. The power it has to move you. The power it has to make you smile. The power it has to make you remember. When I first heard *Flies on the Butter* by Wynonna Judd, I had to pull my car over so I could cry. No joke. I know I joke a lot, but that is the honest truth. The gospel truth, as my family would say.

The song made me remember. It made me remember what happened before life became tainted with well, life. With never ending deadlines and a mind that doesn't know how to shut off. It made me remember a time before love broke the heart and broken promises crushed the soul. It made me remember a time before responsibilities and mortgages. But it also let me me remember a time that if at all possible I would on many given days, when demands ensue, transport myself once again, to a world of Chinese Freeze-tag, the ice cream man and his pitiful sounding music, to a world before you had to watch for predators or walk home in groups. To a perfect time.

I'd learned long before I heard those lyrics that you can't go home again, not to the home that you once knew. Even had a rather comical conversation with my mother one night wishing I could just crawl back up into her womb. She wasn't too sure my high heels would fit. But I hope that in the pages of this book you can at least for a moment be transported to the innocence of a life that once was, and realize that there is always redemption for the life that now is.

Many thanks to the Thomas Nelson team—Allen, Heather, Natalie, Jennifer—for believing in the voice that I have come to develop even on days when I'm not sure there is anything left to say.

To Mark Ross—you created one more beautiful cover.

To Ami McConnell—I love your talent, I love your e-mails, and I love the fact that you really love this book.

To Laura Wright—thank you for extending your beautiful talents my way.

To Marjory Wentworth—thank you for your tireless efforts, endless energy, and wonderful abilities.

acknowledgments

To James Hodgin and David McCullom—thank you for believing in this vision and carrying it out as your own.

To the songwriters—thank you for allowing people like me to be taken away by the power of a song.

You Can't Go Home Again (Flies on the Butter) Words and Music by Allen Shamblin, Austin Cunningham, and Chuck Cannon Copyright © 1998 by Famous Music LLC, Song Matters, Inc., Built On Rock Music, and Wacissa River Music, Inc. All rights for Song Matters, Inc. administered by Famous Music LLC. All rights for Built On Rock Music administered by ICG. All rights for Wacissa River Music, Inc. administered by BPJ Administration, P.O. Box 218061, Nashville, TN 37221-8061. International copyright secured. All rights reserved.

To my family—Thank you for giving me some of my most wonderful memories. It has been a joy to spend this last year thumbing through them again in my mind. I only hope my children will be able to one day do the same with theirs. You are my greatest treasures.

To my friends—I would name you all again—but I believe I left a few out last time, so you know who you are. You are priceless to me. You as well have given me so many wonderful memories through this journey of life.

acknowledgments

To my husband—You are a part of my best memories. Even though we've had many painful ones along the way, they have brought us to an extraordinary place. And to finish out this life and its memories, there's no one else I'd want to do that with than you.

To my savior, Jesus Christ—I have to say—that I'm glad you're not so great at remembering. I'm glad that you can forget as far as the east is from the west. And I'm glad that you remember what matters most: the depth of my love for you.

And to the reader—I know this is a far piece, as we say in the South, from what you have come to be familiar with when picking up one of my books. However, sister needed to know that she could write about something other than crazy people from the South. Didn't work out real well, because I just found another group of crazies! But my hope through this book is that our journey together affords you the ability to unearth some memories of your own. May most make you smile. And even if some make you cry, take a moment to forgive or to let someone forgive you. And after you've finished laughing or crying, don't forget to swat good and hard at those flies on the butter!

Blessings,
Denise

Reading Group Guide

1. The line from the song says, "You can dream about it every now and then. But you can't go home again." What does "home" represent in this story? Have you ever felt as though you couldn't "go home" again?

2. Rose feels as if everything in her life has to be perfect and of high quality—her home, her food, her clothes, her car, her marriage. What do you think she is trying to cover up with the perception of a perfect life? How does the pressure of having a "perfect life" haunt her?

3. The characters of Granddaddy and Mamaw are so central and grounding for many of the other characters in the story. In what ways do you think these two most influence their children and grandchildren?

4. Rose's need to be in control permeates every area of her life. Why do you think she always needs to be in control? Can you identify with Rose's need for control in your own life?

5. Why do you think Rose doesn't want to have child Why does she hide that fear from Jack?

6. How would you describe Rose's relationship with Charlotte? With Christopher?

7. Why do you think it makes Rose so upset to be called "irritable"?

8. Rose feels as if no one—not even Jack—*really* knows her. Why do you think she is so restless in her identity? How does Rose prevent others from really knowing her? In what ways can you identify with Rose's struggle with identity?

9. Why do you think Rose gave in to an affair with Richard? What do you think she was looking for?

10. Do you think that Rose wanted to be honest with Jack? If so, what held her back? Why didn't Rose think Jack could forgive her?

ose refuses to forgive her mother's affair, yet she chooses me destructive path for herself. Do you think Rose's deal with her mother's affair influenced her choices?

the company of family allows you to see the the bad in yourself—as if looking into a ink Rose has chosen to distance her- geographically and emotionally?

13. In this book, Rose embarks on a journey home—both literally and spiritually. Along the way, many people influence her journey. What roles did Herschel, Daisy the waitress, Pastor Lionel, and Abigail play in Rose's journey home?

14. Why do you think Rose needed to hear, and was moved by, Abigail's retelling of the story of Joseph?

15. What do you think is the significance of the title, *Flies on the Butter?*

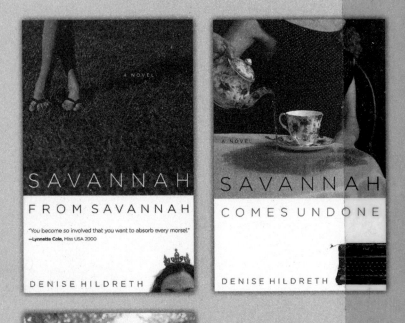
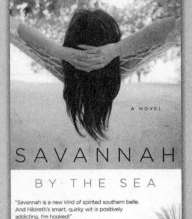